A TALE OF TIME

978-1-7397401-0-8
KhalisHouse Publishing

www.KhalisHouse.com
info@KhalisHouse.com

Find us on:
Instagram/KhalisHouse
Twitter/KhalisHouse

Khalis House
Publishing
Read today. Lead tomorrow.

For my parents, Jagpal Singh and Parmjit Kaur, who told me I could do anything, and for Upjeet Kaur, who taught me that Sikhi is love, and inspired this story.

by Harmanjit Kaur Sidhu

Part One: Oxford, Present Day

CHAPTER ONE

Where are you really from?

'Where are you from?'

Raj pretended not to hear the question, which was hard because he and Lewis were the only two people in the room. Lewis was the oldest employee in the university's administrative building. He was almost completely bald and bony – his wrists and elbows straining painfully against his almost translucent skin. He was somewhat of a legend around the office, but Raj knew this was more endearment than an actual admiration of his abilities, which Raj knew left a lot to be desired. Raj had spent most of his first few weeks fixing Lewis' spreadsheet entries and trying to teach him how to use Excel properly. They'd avoided discussing anything personal, though, and that was the only thing Raj liked about spending every day of his entire summer holiday in this tiny, airless room, within easily the ugliest building in the whole of Oxford.

Raj had caught Lewis staring nervously at his turban a few times over the last few days. He'd felt extra self-conscious about tucking his small antique *kirpan* (sword) into his shirt before coming into the office each morning.

Lewis took in a long, wheezy breath as though he was going to say something else, so Raj quickly replied, 'Southall, West London.'

Lewis grunted in response.

Wait for it … thought Raj.

'Where are you *really* from?' Lewis asked.

Bingo.

'My parents are from Punjab, if that's what you mean.' Raj replied.

'Oh … and your …' Lewis gestured awkwardly to the air around his own head.

Raj wished he could sink deeper into his chair and then all the way through the floor. He was so tired. Exhaustion was creeping into his bones like a slowly advancing cold. Getting out of bed felt like an even bigger challenge than usual these days. This unnatural tiredness was what made him crave a quiet day of spreadsheet entry with the only soundtrack being Lewis' wheezy breath in the background, and now that plan was well and truly thwarted.

'I wear it as a sign of my faith.'

Short and simple, he thought. Lewis was looking at him as though he expected him to continue, so Raj gave a disjointed, possibly even factually incorrect, explanation about why Sikhs wore turbans. He delivered the short speech without really connecting to anything he was saying. He understood what Lewis was really asking, which was why would you even bother, and Raj wasn't sure he knew the answer to that question either, at least not anymore. He tied his dastaar (turban) every morning because it was just a part

2

of who he was, and not wearing it would mean more stares at his long, uncut hair, and cutting his hair would mean yet even more questions.

Also, Roop would never forgive him if he cut his hair. It was an expensive relationship with her sometimes. He got her support, fierce loyalty, and good sense of humour, but it necessitated putting up with her long, one-eyebrow-raised stares if he told her he didn't want to go to a Sikh Society event or meet their friends for dinner, or if he confessed to not doing any of his nitnem (he had learned his lesson on that one and not admitted it again). He didn't like letting her down because she was the only one who understood when the waves of darkness hit him and how to get him out of them. When he told her he had finally been prescribed anti-depressant medication, she just asked him what the dosage was and made him put a reminder into his phone so he didn't miss one.

Lewis had lapsed back into silence, and Raj allowed himself to relax. Only a few more hours to go, and then he would be heading to the last Sikh Society meeting of the term. He was dreading the social interaction but looking forward to saying goodbye to all of them as they left university at the end of the summer term. Then it would be just him and Roop hanging around Oxford for the summer. Raj had wanted to avoid being at home, so he had taken the first summer job he had found, and Roop was trying to save money for her mum's cancer treatment. Lewis shuffled over with his old ledger, and Raj sighed, pulling up Excel so he could fix all Lewis' calculations.

Raj knew the Sikh society meeting had been a bad idea. He had arrived late on purpose, taking a detour through university parks, dawdling by the covered market. When he eventually got to the college buildings and found the room location that Roop had texted him, the Sikh Soc meeting was well underway. He ducked into the room, deliberately looking down at his shoes so he could get to his usual seat at the back without the pain of making small talk. Nobody noticed him; they were in the middle of a spirited argument, which Raj had heard thousands of times already.

'But if we just made it a small thing, at a local club–'

'We are not doing a night out – I told you this before, it goes totally against Sikh values and–'

'Don't be such an extremist–'

'Yeah, who made you the expert on Sikh values?' shouted Taran. Raj noticed he was wearing a new snapback; he wanted to knock it off suddenly. He looked to the Sikh Soc president, Kirpal Singh, and thought maybe he felt the same.

Raj sunk deeper into the back bench, wishing he had remembered to bring his headphones. It took an effort to gaze around the room; there weren't many people in Sikh Soc anymore, which was why Roop made him go every time. They'd had more members when they were still organising things like speed dating events, but that was before Kirpal the Extremist became president. The door to the lecture room opened again, and this time Roop bustled in, swinging her long plait over her shoulder. If his entrance had been

4

understated, Roop made sure to slam the door loudly to announce her arrival.

'Roop!' said Kirpal with relief, 'can you please explain why we can't organise a night out for the incoming freshers?'

'Why do we always end up talking about the same things?' said Roop wearily. 'Let's do the Q & A like we planned.'

'Excellent idea,' said Kirpal, rolling up his sleeves. 'Let's get started; who wants to go first?'

Roop made her way over to Raj. He found himself wishing she had chosen somewhere else to sit because she always created a new centre-of-the-room wherever she went, and now the limelight was on him too.

'Yo! Raj! I didn't even see you!' It was Taran, yelling from the front of the room. 'Are you good, bro?'

A few of the others exchanged nervous glances, and Raj wished for the second time that he could disappear. Grief was like carrying around the weight of a second body sometimes, one that nobody else could see.

'He's fine,' said Roop firmly. 'Can we get back to the questions?'

'OK, everyone, any questions about Sikhi, any at all – I'll try my best to answer.' called Kirpal from the front of the room.

'How much do you want a bet that the first one is going to be about why Nihang Singhs can eat meat but other Sikhs can't?' whispered Roop in his ear. Raj felt himself smiling despite himself, his face hurting with the unfamiliarity of it.

'No, it's going to be – why can Sikhs cut their nails but not cut their hair?' Raj replied.

Roop sniggered. A few minutes passed. One of the girls at the front of the room had asked a question, but Raj drowned it out, tried to concentrate on a fixed point in the ceiling, and hoped this would make the time go by quicker.

'Raj!' Roop elbowed him painfully in the ribs.

'What?'

'Stop doing that zoning out thing … How's things with your parents?'

'Mum packed all of Dad's things last night, told him to find somewhere else to stay.'

'Woah.'

'He was the one driving the car.'

'Raj …'

'I know what you're going to say.'

'Just that you should speak to someone.'

'Won't make my little brother any less dead, will it? Anyways, I'm taking my pills.'

Roop opened her mouth to say something, but Raj felt a tide of exhaustion, which felt almost unbearable, and so he stood up.

'I'm going to head back home, actually.'

Roop looked hurt before shrugging. 'If you want.'

He turned away from her. Nobody else noticed him leave.

He didn't want to go home, and he had already given up his college room for the term. Back in Southall, his mum would be at a yoga or Zumba class, and his dad would be drinking with his friends. The house would be dark, cold, empty. He had tried to speak to his parents a bit more, make some effort to fill that massive, gaping hole of death whenever he wasn't staying at university, but he wasn't Bhagat, and he never would be. After Bhagat's death, the new status quo involved the whole family avoiding each other as much as possible.

Sometimes, when Raj felt at his darkest, he wondered whether his parents had wished that Bhagat had been the son that had survived the accident, not him. Bhagat had, after all, been the funny, lively, kind one and Raj the depressed, sad, studious one. There was no replacing him or the void he had left behind, so Raj learned to stop trying.

He wandered around town for a while, stopping to watch kids trying to skate in front of the business school building next to the station. There was a guy with a blond mohawk who kept helping a younger boy back to his feet after every failed attempt at performing a trick over the raised pavement. Raj watched them for a little while, but then he realised, suddenly, that they were brothers. It felt like it always did– like the Earth was shifting on its axis, as though the pain would make him blind. He felt the finality of it, the rock bottom, which always seemed to get deeper and lower. He turned away from the scene and began to walk. He hadn't realised where he was going until he came up to the front of the building.

Pitt Rivers Museum had always been Raj's favourite place in Oxford. A place where the past was still unfolding around him, where it was still possible to see the ceremonial robes of a people that no longer existed, where one might see a coin that had changed the fate of its owner, or the weapon that had served a soldier until his final battle cry. His favourite item was discovered during a Sikh Soc trip in his first year at the university – a set of *chakrams* owned by a Nihang Singh, engraved in *gurmukhi* script. The circular steel quoits had stirred something in him, back then, made him think that maybe his presence there was not by coincidence, as though there was a much bigger design at play. He had never met the Nihang Singh who had owned that *chakram*, but despite the hundreds of years that separated them, they now had Oxford in common.

The *chakrams* had inspired him so much he had spent most of his first-year maintenance grant on an antique dagger, which he wore on his *gatra* around his neck. He had been more connected then to Sikhi, his physics degree, and the other members of the Sikh Society. Then his brother was killed in a car accident, turning everything he knew into an upside-down version of reality. The *kirpan* still felt reassuring, though, bumping against his hip as he wondered the narrow pathways between rows and rows of time.

The museum was supposed to be closed at this time, but Pitt Rivers had been his first job when he arrived at the university. He spent most of his first year selling pencils and magnets in the small souvenir shop next to the entrance, and he'd made good friends with Lukas, the night security guard. He was sure Lukas still let him come and go as he pleased because of what had happened to Bhagat, but he didn't care – he was happy to play the grief card where necessary.

He climbed the stairs to the top floor and stood in front of the dusty glass cabinet with the chakrams inside. It didn't feel quite the same, though; in fact, the more Raj paid attention to that feeling, it grew. It felt as though someone was watching him – like he wasn't alone.

He turned around slowly; the corridor behind him was deserted. He felt unease creeping up his back like a hand, and he shivered a little.

Get a grip, Raj. He said to himself, holding his *kirpan* a little tighter. He walked around the circular structure of the third floor, looking down into the middle of the building, where the ground floor was visible. There was no one there. He took a deep breath and came back to the *chakrams*. He wondered briefly if he could get away with spending the night there, and that's when he felt a hand on his shoulder.

CHAPTER TWO

An intersection

Raj turned around suddenly, almost losing his balance. The man reached out both hands to steady him. Raj could only stare at this stranger. He was a Singh, with a white, wispy beard, which grew all the way past and under a thick leather belt. His turban was big and blue, and he was wrapped in a long and heavy-looking leather coat, with multiple silver fastenings, each of them jingling slightly as he helped straighten Raj.

'Steady on, young man!' He smiled, revealing brilliantly white teeth.

'The museum is closed–' began Raj.

'I know, but I needed a place to go,' interrupted the old man.

'A place to go?' repeated Raj

'Yeah, everyone needs one of those, right? A place to just exist, to be? Not many of those left in this time period,' said the man, smiling at him again.

'Time period?'

The man cocked his head to one side playfully. 'Are you just going to keep repeating everything I say? Everyone is a bit obsessed with time, aren't they? Most people waste it while worrying if it is going to run out. Never made sense to me.'

'But how did you get into the museum?'

'I have ways of getting just about anywhere.' he responded.

The man's gaze fell on Raj's waist.

'That's a nice *kirpan*,' the man said suddenly, and Raj saw that his gatra had come loose in the rush to leave the Sikh Soc meeting. His antique kirpan glinted in the dim light.

'I've seen it before, but that was many years ago. I've actually been waiting for this moment for a while, this intersection.' continued the man.

'Intersection?'

The man's mouth twitched, and Raj realised he was repeating his words back at him again.

'The intersection – my path with yours. It was written this way.'

Raj scoffed. 'Written that way? You honestly believe that?'

The man smiled at him; there was no confrontation in his expression, and it seemed as though he wanted Raj to carry on speaking, so he did.

'People cling to the idea of fate because the alternative – the reality – is too scary to comprehend – the idea that suffering can be random and without reason, that one day you can be standing next to someone you love so much, and the next day they can be gone forever frightens people. Bad things happen to good people all the time, and we talk about fate and *Karam* and *Kismat* because we want a way of understanding them – we don't want to believe that suffering is as inevitable as it is useless. People are not brave, so we

11

talk about things being written, each event having a reason behind it, and we hope that will be enough to let us wake up the next day, to carry on.'

Raj finished and then looked down at his feet, feeling embarrassed suddenly. He hadn't meant to say that much.

'You don't think there's any order to the chaos?'

'I think people spend their lives trying to find order where there is none because human nature is to try and rationalise everything.'

'But not you – you think you've overcome the deception of it. Are you happy now?'

Raj shrugged. 'Well, I am now on anti-depressants; take from that what you will.'

The man laughed at that. 'You like coming here, though, don't you? Why do you think that is?'

Raj blinked; he hadn't considered this before. 'I don't know.'

The man gave him an almost disappointed-looking smile, and Raj felt like he had let down a teacher.

'I think it's because the past is fixed,' said Raj suddenly, without fully knowing where the words were coming from. 'We already know what's happened, and some of it was hard, and some of it was good, but it's done, and there's no more uncertainty anymore. Whereas the future …'

'I've got something that I think you will find interesting … I'm a bit of a fan of history myself, actually.' said the man.

He took off a black rucksack that Raj had not noticed before. He rummaged around in it for a while, and Raj shifted awkwardly from one foot to the other. This was definitely not how he had expected this night to go.

Finally, the man pulled out a plastic folder with a small, battered-looking leather notebook inside. He reached inside carefully and turned to a page at the centre of the book. Raj took it and stared at the writing confusedly; it was written in a cramped, messy script. He could just about make out a few letters of Gurmukhi.

'What is this?'

'It's an old account – written by a Sikh, where he's talking about a battle with some Turks in a forest near Lahore. 18th century – dire times for the Sikhs, as I am sure you will know.'

'Wow … I didn't realise anything like this existed.'

The man nodded. 'It's an extremely rare find. I was lucky to get my hands on it.'

'How can you be sure this is real? It looks like it's in really good condition.'

'My sources are reliable on this, I think. Shall I tell you what it says?'

Raj nodded eagerly.

'It does go on a bit – I'm afraid that this particular Singh was a fan of embellishment, there are some tall tales in this book – but the climatic bit is right at the end. They are about to lose this particular fight, all the Singhs, and some Kaurs, are lying dead or injured outside the fort, and just when the enemy thinks they have won – one last Singh stands up to fight and manages to rally the last of Sikh resistance. The description is mostly quite generic – beard, blue turban, except for the bit about the man's *kirpan* – the author writes that it has two bejewelled peacocks on it.'

Raj looked down at the *kirpan* hanging on his gatra, the antique *kirpan*, which the seller had promised had seen actual battles once upon a time … the antique *kirpan* with the two silver peacocks facing each other, right near the hilt.

'No way.'

The man's eyes twinkled a little, and for a second, Raj thought he looked almost other-worldly. As though if Raj reached out to touch him, he would find nothing but air.

'Does our meeting sound like it was written now?'

Raj opened his mouth to respond, but then suddenly, he heard the sound of footsteps on the stairs leading up to their floor.

'Did you bring other people with you?'

The man sighed. 'Not intentionally; they've been following me all over Oxford today. That's the reliable thing about people; throughout the ages, they'll always fear what they don't understand.'

'Who are you people?' asked Raj, slowly backing away from the man and towards the entrance to the stairs. He thought about making a break for it and then realised there was no way of getting out if the stairs were blocked.

'They're making my job a whole lot harder than it has to be,' continued the man. 'I think we should start running now. Trust me; you don't want them to catch you here, now that they know you've spoken to me.'

The man turned on his heel and began speed-walking towards an unmarked door a few metres away from the chakrams, which Raj had never paid attention to. He considered for a moment and then thought his chances at taking on the old man in a fight were probably better than facing whoever was climbing up those stairs.

Raj followed the man's half-jog down a set of stairs, and they wound up in an alleyway between the museum building and the department of biochemistry. The roads were totally empty now; most students had found their beds for the night.

'Stay out of the light,' commanded the old man, pulling Raj by the arm to move closer to the huge bins lining one side of the alley.

'Okay, that's enough!' said Raj finally. The old man was almost a foot taller than him and surprisingly fast. Raj fought to catch his breath, stopping to lean against the wall for support. They had almost reached university parks, and Raj had no desire to head into a deserted park with this man and their potential assailants.

'Who the hell are you?'

'I'm going to help you find your way.' replied the man simply.

'I'm not lost.'

The man smiled. 'Everyone is lost, in one way or another. All of us out here, just trying to get back home.'

Raj didn't know what to say to that.

'I wanted to give you a gift,' the man continued, reaching into his bag again. From it, he pulled …

'Is that a *chakram*?! Hang on; this is THE *chakram*! Did you steal it from the museum?'

The man smiled. 'The museum stole it first. This was simply a recovery.'

'I can't keep this!'

The man held a finger to his lips. 'They're catching up with us again.'

He pulled Raj further into a shadowy alcove of a disused side entrance to a department building.

'That's the government. They've never really believed me when I told them I wasn't a threat. A harmless old man like me, and they send their best agents.'

'Are you a thief?'

'I'm a traveller, Raj Singh, and I came to give you the *chakram.* When the time is right, its purpose will be revealed to you. At the moment, you're not ready, so we can't take the journey into the past together. All I can tell you is that the lesson will disappear once it has been learned. Oh, and keep a look out for the Baaj – it will take you home if you ask nicely.'

Raj opened his mouth again, but the man had already slipped out of the shopfront archway and merged into the night's shadowy darkness. It was only then he realised that the man had known his name without him ever giving it.

CHAPTER THREE

An Escape from Oxford

Raj was being followed. Usually, he would have dismissed these thoughts as paranoia, or side effects of medication, or his brain playing tricks on him the way it was prone to do these days, but after last night (which he could have sworn was a dream had it not been for the *chakram* in his bag right now) he was less confident of this.

It had started as soon as Raj had got off the train at Oxford Station when he noticed a man in a pinstriped suit watching him over the edge of his newspaper. It was laughably cliche to believe that he was a spy, so Raj ignored his original instincts to go and hide in the station toilet and instead continued his commute to Wellington Street. But there was the man again as he crossed the road by Worcester College, and then another man in a tweed jacket stood by the Sadler library, watching him intently. Raj was grateful for the foot traffic of tourists and the last of the students who had yet to make their way back home for the summer. He was sure this was to do with his meeting with the strange man yesterday and potentially the *chakram*, which bumped against his shoulder blades with each step he took.

He didn't know what to do. He resisted the urge to jog the rest of the way to the relative safety of the administrative building, where they wouldn't admit anyone without an ID card. It was only when he beeped in his card through the main entrance and began climbing the stairs that he wondered if he'd made a mistake in leading the strange men directly to his workplace. What if they were waiting for him when he finished work? What did they want from him? He was going to take the *chakram* back; of course, he was. He just had to think of a way of doing it that didn't involve him getting arrested for theft.

Lewis was boiling water in a grimy, off-white kettle by the window, looking out onto Wellington Square. Raj was too scared to creep up to the window next to him and see whether the men were indeed waiting to grab him as he left the building. He collapsed into the ancient wheely chair instead, its tired springs whining in protest.

Lewis looked over from the kettle. 'What's wrong with you?'

'Long night.'

Lewis grunted. 'There are two suits hanging out near the front of the building; they look a bit lost.'

Raj gulped, his worst fears confirmed.

'Lewis, do you know if there's another exit from this building?'

Lewis frowned at him, the kettle beeped to confirm it was boiled, and the sound made Raj jump.

'You can exit via the IT building – but are you going to tell me what the issue is? Is someone bothering you?'

Raj hesitated; he hadn't expected Lewis to be so observant or probing – he certainly wasn't on most days, but when Raj caught his reflection in Lewis' polished steel plaque 'employee of the month 1991' he saw he looked terrible. His skin was pallid, his under-eye dark circles even more pronounced, his dastaar felt loose, tied haphazardly in the morning.

'You see those men in suits outside? I think they might be looking for me.'

Lewis raised his eyebrows sceptically. 'And why would they be interested in someone like you?'

Raj was quiet for a little while, and Lewis took the opportunity to pour hot water into a mug. Raj was surprised when he shuffled over to put it in front of him.

'Get some tea in you and calm down.'

Raj nodded gratefully and sipped the tea. It did work, weirdly, the heat washing through his chest and helping to settle his empty, but somehow still churning, stomach. Raj tried to act like the men outside the building no longer phased him, and Lewis seemed to buy it as the rest of the morning went by in their normal routine – Lewis filling out the accounts in the ledger and Raj inputting them sheet by sheet into the computer, correcting as he went.

'Right, I'm off to eat lunch outside,' said Lewis, stretching his short arms. Raj hated it when he did this; it made the translucent skin of his forearms stretch so far that it became almost transparent.

Once Lewis had left, Raj walked slowly over to the window. The square was empty apart from other university employees taking advantage of the sunshine and laying out picnics over the green space at the centre of the square. Not a suit in sight. Raj breathed out a shaky breath and pulled out his phone to do what he had wanted to do since the man had first appeared behind him in Pitt River Museum – he texted Roop.

A few hours later, Raj stood pressed against the stone archway of a closed antiques shop, sweat trickling down his back. The position offered him the perfect line of sight to the entrance of Oxford train station and a bit of respite from the now blaring July afternoon sun. He watched as the same black Audi circled the ring road for the third time; he was still being followed.

He checked the time on his phone. Roop's train had arrived. Two minutes later, he saw Roop impatiently battling fellow passengers, most of them lost-looking tourists, and making her way down the station stairs. He waited until she had crossed the ring road before texting her his location.

'Raj? Why are you hiding?' He heard her voice before he saw her.

He pulled her into the alcove.

'I'm not hiding … can you see that Audi, on the main road?'

'Yes. What about it?'

'You're not going to believe what happened last night.'

'I swear to God, Raj, this had better be good. I had to leave Mum with the Macmillan nurse she doesn't like.'

'The one who keeps trying to get her to wear healing crystals?' asked Raj, momentarily distracted.

'Mum was not happy.'

'Let's go somewhere quiet.'

'I know just the place,' said Roop, making to step back onto the street. Raj grabbed her arm and pulled her back into the alcove.

'Ouch!'

'Sorry, Roop, but look – the Audi is doing another loop.'

They watched as the shiny black car drove slowly past them, the windows were tinted, but Raj still suppressed a shiver at the thought of those two men.

Roop watched as the car slipped out of sight, then she took Raj's hand, and they stepped into the street.

He should have known Roop would choose their home college. They took a random, winding route through numerous back streets at an almost half- sprint to St John's, Raj admiring Roop's navigational abilities. They seemed to have lost the Audi, though Raj still felt a prickly sensation on the back of his neck as though they were still being watched. He sighed in relief as they flashed their student ID badges to the surly porter at the entrance. He raised his eyebrow at them both.

'Can you please not run inside the college building?'

Roop nodded, too out of breath to speak, flicking her long hair away from her face and neck.

They found their way to the old library, and Roop was right – it was the last place anyone in their right mind would be in the first week of summer term. Raj shrugged off his backpack, feeling his T-shirt stick to his back with sweat unpleasantly.

Roop tossed her hair over a shoulder again and looked at him impatiently. Raj reached into his bag and pulled out the *chakram*.

'You brought a *chakram*? Are you going to start wearing it? Might be slightly alarming for Lewis, but I support–'

'No,' said Raj. 'This isn't just a *chakram*, it's one of THE *chakrams* at Pitt River Museum.'

Raj shared the details of his late-night encounter. Roop leaned back onto an ancient wooden desk, and Raj jumped when it creaked loudly.

'So wait, there's a bunch of random people after you because they think you stole the *chakram*? Are they the police?'

'I don't know!' said Raj. 'I want to take this back – but I don't know how to explain what happened.'

'Don't they have CCTV? You could just tell the truth and–'

'It's too risky, and Lukas could get in big trouble for letting me in!'

'Well, we could go to the police station together and–'

'And say what? A Sikh dumbledore appeared in front of me yesterday and seemed to know my name and told me I was soon going on a magical mission and then forced me to steal a priceless artefact that I've been carrying around in my bag all day while running away from strange government men driving Audis?!'

'You don't need to take that tone with me – I'm only trying to help!'

'Roop, I'm freaking out here!'

She bit her lip.

'I hate it when you do that.' said Raj angrily. 'Just come out and say what you want to say.'

'You're on some pretty strong medication, so I'm only going to ask you this once – but do you think there's a chance you might be mis-remembering some of what happened yesterday?'

He sighed. The worst part about having any kind of mental health issue wasn't that people asked you whether things were all in your head; it was that you started questioning it too. It had felt real – but so had other things in the past – like a conversation with his brother, which had turned out to be a dream, or that time he could have sworn he felt Bhagat's hand in his own when he was walking home from the station, even though they hadn't held hands in a long time. Grief, depression, and anxiety did that to your mind, creating new realities, some of which felt good enough to want to live in forever.

'It's real, Roop. It felt different.'

'OK,' said Roop, standing up from the desk. 'It happened. So what's next? You can't spend your whole life hiding. I say we confront them–'

'What?!'

'–there's two of us, and we're in broad daylight, and they will–'

'No. Look, you didn't see the way the guy reacted to them last night … if he's running, then so am I.'

Roop considered him for a moment. 'Fine. What do we do then?'

'There was something else he said – something about the purpose of the chakram being revealed to me, and that I would undertake a journey into the past – and that if I asked nicely, a Baaj would take me home?'

Roop was silent. The sun shifted slightly, putting her into a half-shadow. Raj watched the sun light up dust particles floating softly through the room; the environment was in a peace that was in total contrast to the turmoil of his mind.

'None of that makes any sense whatsoever.'

'Tell me about it.'

Roop stood up and started pacing, something she did whenever working out a particularly tricky problem. Raj put the backpack on again, not wanting to be far from the *chakram* for some inexplicable reason.

'He was talking to you about an ancient historical account – some kind of diary kept by a Sikh in the mid-1700s.'

'Correct.'

'I've never heard of any account of that nature. Sounds almost implausible that something like that would have been produced, let alone preserved to such a high degree.'

Roop was a history student; he should have known that would have felt like the most implausible part of the interaction to her.

'So you think it was fake?'

'I don't think he is messing with you – why would he? I think he believes the things he is saying … it sounds like you're about to have some kind of adventure. And until you have it, there's not a whole lot we can do except lay low …'

Suddenly, Raj felt a dull buzzing in the centre of his back.

'What's that sound?' asked Roop. 'Is your phone on vibrate?'

Raj slid off his rucksack again and opened the zip with shaky fingers. The *chakram* was vibrating …

He looked up at Roop and caught sight of her similarly puzzled expression. Suddenly, the sound of arguing voices came through the old wooden library door – without quite knowing why, he took hold of the *chakram* and Roop's hand. They looked towards the door as two men in dark suits came bursting through the old entrance, and Raj felt a sharp, pure fear in his heart as one of them looked at him directly in the eyes, and then everything went black.

Part 2: Punjab, 1750s

CHAPTER FOUR

Homecoming

The first thing Raj felt was the dampness of the grass on his back, bleeding through the thin material of his T-shirt. He wanted to move, but each limb felt like it had doubled in heaviness. He opened his eyes and blinked a few times, but only pitch-black darkness greeted him, so thick and impenetrable that he questioned whether he had actually opened his eyes at all. He sat up carefully, taking deep breaths against the feeling of suffocation.

As his eyes adjusted, he could make out a canopy of trees above and the faint suggestions of moonlight falling unevenly in the clearing around him.

'Roop?' he whispered into the darkness, feeling afraid of breaking the silence of this place.

He felt in his pocket for his phone – no service, but the torchlight allowed him to make out another shape a few metres from him, also stirring.

'Raj? Where the hell are we?!' said Roop.

He stood up and went over to help her to her feet.

'I don't remember anything except grabbing your hand.'

'Lie down on the ground! Drop your weapons!'' a shout in Punjabi went out.

The sound of hooves shattered the silence of the clearing, and within seconds he knew they were surrounded. Raj's phone fell from his hand as somebody pushed him to the ground. He hit the grass hard, felt his tooth sink into the bottom of his lip as he shouted.

'Stop!' Raj yelled in Punjabi. 'We're not trying to hurt anyone!'

'Veer Ji – they look like Sikhs to me,' said one of the men, dismounting from his horse. He stepped into the light from Raj's phone – a Singh with a tall blue turban, armed with two long kirpans.

The man he was speaking to also dismounted. He was older; his long, wild beard flecked with more white and grey than black.

Roop tried to say something.

'Silence! Who are you, and where have you come from?' shouted the older man.

The third and final member of the ambush cantered forward on his horse. He looked like the youngest of the group, and he wore a white turban, his hands wrapped around a long mala. He addressed the older man.

'We need to move right now; the enemy is on our tails.'

'We can't just leave them here,' the first man said.

'Tie them up and get them onto the horses. And pick up that candle–'

Raj looked down to where the man was gesturing – his phone. He opened his mouth to protest, to explain, but the younger men were already grabbing them; he felt the tightening of a rope around his torso.

27

'Wait, please – we're just trying to get home–'

'What are these coarse trousers you are wearing?' asked the white-turbaned man curiously, patting Raj's jeans. 'They look very uncomfortable.'

'Don't touch me!' screamed Roop from next to them; the man with the two swords picked her up and put her onto his horse.

'We're not going to hurt you,' he said, holding his hands up. 'We're taking you back to camp to ask a few more questions. That is all.'

'Move, now!' the older man shouted, and they scrambled onto the horses. Raj gripped onto the man in front of him for dear life as the horse began to canter and then gallop, the cool night wind whipping his face. All around him, there was only darkness – silent and impenetrable. *A journey into the past,* the old man had said; *surely not*, thought Raj.

They arrived at what appeared to be a campsite a while later. Raj couldn't be sure how long they had been riding for; his mind was a storm of thoughts, anxiety gripping his chest like a vice tighter than the ropes he had been bound with. The site was a bigger clearing in the forest than the one they had been captured in. A small, dying fire had been lit in its centre; the glowing embers allowed Raj to make out fraying tent-like buildings around the edges of the clearing and the shape of more horses tied to trees on the far side of the fire. They stamped their hooves noisily as the men disembarked and pulled down Raj and Roop.

'Roop?' he whispered.

'Raj, do you think we just went back in time?'

'Tell us who you are!' said the older man, pulling them both roughly near the dying fire.

Raj looked at Roop, and they arrived at another one of their unspoken agreements – *lie.*

'My name is Roop, and this is my brother Raj,' said Roop quickly. 'We were travelling with our family but got separated because …'

'We were attacked – don't know who it was, it was dark,' Raj added. 'Our horses were stolen, and we got separated.'

'When you found us, we were just resting … we've been trying to find our family.'

'A Sikh family? Travelling during these troubled times? What did you expect?' said the old man harshly. Her made-up story had evidently elicited no sympathy from him. He stood directly next to the fire, arms crossed, the fading flames casting shadows across his face, highlighting the harsh planes of his cheekbones and the fierceness of his beard.

Raj wondered what period they had landed in – Sikhs living in the forest, the mention of enemies, the worn and ragged look of the warriors in front of him. It could only be the 1750s – an era of invasions and bloodshed. He gulped. How on Earth were they going to get back home?

'Yes, we should have been more careful. If you let us leave, we can be on our way–'

'It's not safe.' The white-turbaned man stepped forward. 'Especially for a young woman. We can't let you leave.'

'He's right – they are our responsibility now,' agreed the other younger man in the blue turban.

The older man evidently had all the authority on this matter, and he regarded them both suspiciously. 'And what if they are both spies, working for the authorities to identify our location? How do we know they won't turn us in at the first opportunity they get?'

The other two men looked at each other with uncertainty.

'We're not spies –' said Roop.

'You can understand why that's not the most convincing defence,' the older man replied. 'But either way, we can't let you leave. Get them both a space to sleep – away from everyone else. And someone keep an eye on them tonight.'

He turned away, ducking into the biggest tent on the perimeter of the clearing.

'Sorry about Mehtab Singh.' The white-turbaned man grinned at them both. 'We're on high alert since our last skirmish – we lost four people. My name is Resham, by the way, and this is Vikram.'

'Hello, do you think you could untie us?' Raj nervously said.

Resham laughed. 'Of course. Sorry again – about your family too. Where are you from?'

They spoke to him directly, ignoring Roop, struggling to extract herself from the fraying rope tied around her arms. Vikram cleared his throat, handing her a sharp knife to help.

'Sorry to you as well, penji. We're not in the habit of tying up women or manhandling them – please excuse our behaviour.'

'Erm, it's fine. Do you know where we are?' asked Roop.

'A few miles from Lahore,' Vikram said. 'But we don't share our actual location for security reasons …'

'We understand," said Raj. 'You said you're on high alert – do you expect more attacks?'

Resham gestured for them to come over to the base of a large oak tree next door to the half-asleep horses. He began to lay out rough sleeping mats.

'Keep your voices down,' he said. 'People sleeping all around you.'

'We're on our last legs here, to be honest,' said Resham, now setting up his own sleeping mat a few metres away. 'We will be moving out to join another Jatha of Sikhs some miles away. Our numbers have depleted really drastically … just one last mission to go–'

'Let's not go into that. You remember what Mehtab said …' warned Vikram.

'Come on, Vikram Singh, do these kids look like spies?'

Raj wanted to protest at being called a kid; he thought they were probably all near about the same age. Vikram and Resham didn't look older than their early 20s, but he had to admit, his smooth palms looked baby-like next to their weathered, calloused hands. When Resham laughed, premature wrinkles lined the edges of his face. He wondered how long they had been living like this, exposed to the elements, under a near-constant threat of death.

'You can never be too careful. We'll speak to them properly in the morning. Let them sleep.'

'But I wanted to ask about that light ...' Resham said disappointedly.

'Goodnight,' said Vikram firmly to Raj and Roop, pulling Resham away to their own sleeping mats, set up a few metres away.

Once they were out of earshot, and Raj couldn't even be sure if they were - this place was *so* quiet - he turned to Roop. She was sitting on her mat, her head in her hands.

'Roop, are you okay?'

'Am I *okay*? Raj, I'm pretty sure we've gone back 300 years in time, in the middle of probably the worst period of Sikh history – with *no* way of getting home. My mum will be wondering where I am ... and there's no one to help her take her medication!'

'Yeah,' he said, clearing his throat. 'Point taken. The Macmillan nurse will be around, though, right?

'They told me today that Mum doesn't have long left. A couple of months at the most.'

Raj felt his stomach drop, the cold and familiar sensation of grief spilling across his chest.

'I'm so sorry. You didn't even get a chance to say–'

'It's fine,' said Roop stoically. 'I just want to get back to her.'

They sat in silence for a few seconds, and he felt sudden exhaustion creeping over him. The same heaviness in his limbs he had experienced when they had first landed here. It reminded him of the bone-deep tiredness after getting off a long flight.

'Wait ...' said Roop. 'The old man, you said he was talking about a *Baaj* taking us home?'

'He also said we would need to ask it nicely; we're supposed to speak to a bird?'

'I mean, we did just travel backwards in time – I'm willing to try communicating with an animal if it means we might have a chance of getting back.'

Raj lay down on the rough mat, the stuffing in it had worn away with time, and the ground felt uncomfortably hard underneath it. He thought longingly of his bed, in his own college lodging, and the smell of fresh sheets on laundry day. Snores broke his daydream, and he felt guilty suddenly. These Sikhs had been sleeping in the jungles for months, and here he was, thinking of pillows and sheets on his very first day.

'Look, let's stick to our story and go along with whatever they say ... and then we can ask to go our own way, look for a *Baaj*.'

'It's not safe for us out there alone,' said Roop. 'I think we should stick with these guys. We should probably also stick to Punjabi from now on if we want to avoid questions about why we know a language that hasn't technically arrived in the sub-continent yet. And, you need to dump your phone somewhere.

Raj looked away from her and up into the sky for the first time. The campsite was sheltered by a thick canopy of trees, but he could see more stars through the gaps than he had ever seen in his life.

'Roop ... the stars ...'

He remembered his first lesson in GCSE Physics, the year when he decided physics was what he wanted to study when he went to university. The teacher had told him that the stars they were looking at actually existed in the past. *We're looking into the past all the time* she had explained; *the past is still happening.*

Eventually, they fell asleep.

CHAPTER FIVE

Soldiers and Scribes

'The night is drenched in dew, and stars are sparkling. The Saints remain wakeful o see the beautiful night; they are the beloveds of Raam.'

Raj woke to the sound of one of his favourite Shabads; the light of dawn cast the campsite in a soft, ethereal glow. Vikram was the one singing as he fed the horses with what looked like a mixture of grassy weeds and a few grains. Roop was already up, sitting with her arms wrapped around her knees.

'Look,' she said, gesturing to the centre of the campsite. A small fire had been lit and gathered around it were more Sikhs – both men and women huddled together for warmth.

They were doing *Nitnem*; one of them was leading, with the others responding with the next line of the *paat* (prayers). He hadn't seen anyone do *paat* like that before. It was like they were having a conversation.

They got up from their mats; Raj felt the stiff muscles in his back protest as they approached the group carefully. There must have been around twenty of them – their clothes tattered. Raj thought they might have been different colours at one point, but now they looked like different shades of the same sludgy grey. There were a few women, probably the same age as Raj's mum, one of them wore a big blue dastaar wrapped neatly with a small sword tucked in the front. The others were wrapped in thick shawls. Their faces looked radiant, though, in the soft light, and the sounds of their voices were strong and melodic.

Raj couldn't remember the last time he had completed his *Nitnem*. Sometimes, when the guilt was too much, he would put his headphones in and listen to *JapJi sahi*b (fast speed on YouTube) while walking to his first lecture of the day. He felt embarrassed as if the evidence of this was written all over his skin. There were no falcons in sight. For the first time in a long time, Raj thought about his Guru and asked for some help.

Breakfast was served like langar at the Gurdwara. They sat down in a tidy row, and one of the women and another Singh brought out thin Rotis (large flat bread) and watery dhaal (cooked lentils). Raj wondered how to eat his dhaal without a spoon but eventually put the misshapen metal bowl to his mouth and drank it instead. The food tasted strange, perhaps the absence of the spices and flavours he had always taken for granted. His stomach growled with unsatisfied hunger. He wondered, yet again, how they had managed to cope like this for so long.

The other Sikhs were more friendly than Mehtab – they asked about Raj and Roops' family, the name of their village. They kept the details vague. One of the Singhs asked if they had seen any other Sikh families on the way; he had looked hopeful until Raj said he hadn't. His eyes had filled with tears, and he blinked them away furiously, ducking into one of the tents.

'Don't mind him,' said Resham, pulling Raj over to the edge of the campsite a few moments later. 'He was separated from his parents a few months ago too. The poor man thinks they are still alive.'

Raj cleared his throat.

'Sorry – obviously, your family is different – I'm sure they are fine–'

Raj fought the bizarre urge to smile. 'It's OK.'

Resham took him by the arm further away from the campsite, stopping by a small pool of water; it reflected the weak light of the sun, sparkling like diamonds. It was so clear that Raj could see all the way to the bottom.

'I thought you might like to wash up. You can show your sister later, too. I got you some spare clothes so you can get out of those trousers. Are you wearing them as some kind of punishment?'

Raj looked down at his worn jeans and thought maybe Resham had a point.

'Thank you,' said Raj, feeling a little uncomfortable about getting undressed. Resham seemed to sense this and turned away, facing the trees. Raj unbuckled his jeans and slid off his T-shirt. The water was cool but not uncomfortably so, and by the time he was finished, he felt like a human being again. Resham had got him a light grey chola to wear. It was a little tight around the stomach area, something Raj tried not to let impact his self-esteem too much, but otherwise, it was soft, light, and warm.

'Now you really look like one of us!'' said Resham. 'The water is amazing, isn't it? It's so random – like it was made specifically for us.'

'It must be hard … living like this,' said Raj lamely. He knew he was stating the obvious, but his mind couldn't fathom living in the constant state of fear and discomfort that these Sikhs endured.

Resham Singh shrugged. 'Once Bhai Bala and Guru Nanak Dev Ji came across a huge stretch of water. Guru Jee turned to Bhai Bala and asked how they would cross. Bhai Bala replied, saying that those with the Guru as their boat easily cross this world ocean. So what have we really got to be afraid of?'

'I wish I thought that way. I'm always scared of the bad things that could happen.'

Resham shrugged. 'The way I think about it is if things are going to go wrong, it's because it is willed to be that way. Don't fight against the ocean's current, and everything will just … flow'

Raj knew he was talking about *Hukam* and fate, and he found he didn't want to debate about it the way he had with the old man. Instead, he changed the subject.

'And what about your family? How did you end up here?'

'Our village was invaded by some Turks. They kept increasing our taxes, and we couldn't afford it anymore. Then they took my dad … he died on his second day of captivity – he was a teacher, hadn't done a day of manual labour in his life, and they had him working all hours in the field – under the glare of the afternoon sun. I tried to keep the family going, but they soon came knocking … they took everything from me. So I ran to the forests. I wasn't even a Sikh until Mehtab found me.'

'They … killed your family?'

'Yes. In front of me.' Resham pulled out his *kirpan*, almost absent-mindedly, sliding his finger along the edge.

Raj said. 'You must miss your family a lot.'

Resham looked down at his kirpan. 'Of course, I miss my parents every single day, but that's nothing compared to how much I think about my little sister. She always thought I was some kind of hero – even though everyone in my village always told me off for being up to no good. People used to come to my dad and tell him I wouldn't ever amount to anything – but my sister … she used to find everything I did impressive.'

Raj tried to manage the fierce pang of pain that hit him at the very core of his being sometimes when he was reminded very suddenly of Bhagat.

'I had a little brother too, once,' he said softly. He hadn't ever spoken about Bhagat like this. Not even to the therapist who Roop had forced him to go and see. He had sat silently in her tiny office, watching the rain slashing against the windows. He didn't know how to put into words that his whole world had crumbled; no language could do justice to the fact that the world had cruelly taken away the thing that was most important to him.

'Let me show you something,' said Resham. He looked around carefully before reaching into the pocket of his frayed tunic. He pulled out a leather volume – one that Raj had seen before – hundreds of years from now in a dark, empty museum.

'I've not shown anyone here except for Mehtab and Vikram, but I write about things ... So I won't forget them.'

He opened the rough-looking pages and pointed out one of the earliest entries

'It started off with me writing about my sister – her favourite colour, the songs she used to sing, and the conversations we had, just so I remembered. But now, I write about almost everything – just so it's recorded, you know?'

Raj nodded, feeling a little floored by the scale of these connections across time and space. He felt suddenly impossibly and hopelessly insignificant.

'My dad taught me how to read and write when I was young – I was lucky. I'm almost out of this paper and ink, though. I'll have to try and get some more ... sometimes I write about things that haven't happened too, stories; they make me laugh.'

Raj smiled. 'Do you think someone will read it one day, hundreds of years from now?'

Resham laughed out loud at that. 'Who on Earth would be interested in what I have to write?! Like I said, it's mostly for myself – for remembering. Remembering is vital.'

'Wouldn't it be easier to forget sometimes?'

Resham shook his head. 'If I forgot about Basant, then that would mean forgetting the way she made me feel – like I wanted to be better, do better. It's worth the pain of missing her, to have known her and loved her.'

They began to walk back towards the campsite again.

'So where did you get that light from? The one you were holding in your hand – is it a candle or what?'

'Oh, um–'

'Enough chit chat,' called Mehtab suddenly from near the fire. 'We're having a meeting.'

When Raj tried to follow the other Sikhs filing into the main tent, a thick arm blocked his way. He gulped as he looked up into Mehtab's eyes.

'You're not fooling me. There's something strange about you and your sister. I don't trust either of you, but you are wearing the roop of the Khalsa, so I will not spill your blood.'

There was silence.

'Erm, thank you?' said Raj.

Mehtab glared at him for a few more seconds before ducking into the tent.

Raj hurried in after him, joining Roop at the end of the semi-circle formed around Mehtab.

'Vaheguru Ji Ka Khalsa, Vaheguru Ji Ki Fateh.'

The quiet chatter of the group was replaced with the response to Mehtab's greeting.

'We are in high spirits, yes?'

One of the women let out a jakaara, and Vikram and Resham's voices were the loudest in response to the war cry.

'I know I said we would join my uncle's Jatha on the other side of this forest. But in the middle of last night, we had a messenger. He confirmed the rumours – Abdali is travelling back to Kabul. His caravans are filled with his loot – gold, money, gems … and women.'

'Waheguru,' said one of the men softly. 'We cannot let him get away with this.'

'I agree,' said Mehtab, and he started pacing, reminding Raj once again of a predatory animal prowling in a cage. 'A plan has been put in place to rescue these women. By the great general himself.'

The Singhs next to Raj looked at each other excitedly.

'Do they mean … THE general?!' Roop began to whisper in Raj's ear. A thrill went down Raj's spine. Would they really come face to face with the legendary figure?

'But Veer Jee ... our numbers are so depleted as it is. I don't know whether we will survive another encounter with the Afghans,' said a man in a frayed chola; he had a long scar down one side of his face.

'We will vote,' said Mehtab. 'I understand that it has been hard.'

He paused as he looked around the room. Raj saw the bright, alert faces of the Sikhs beside him, but also how weary they were, the frayed clothes, the sharp cheekbones, the broken and dirty heels of their feet.

'But as long as there is breath in my body, I will fight against this tyranny. Even if the odds are against us – especially if they are against us. The Guru trusted us so much he gave us his form and appearance – what face will I show him when one day I return to him; how will I say that I gave up without a fight?'

Mehtab's voice was quieter than before, but he kept pacing up and down the front of the tent; it made Raj's skin erupt in goosebumps.

'Now all those who vote to join the general and stop Abdali, raise your hands.'

Everything was still for a second, and then arms shot up; some of the Sikhs even raised both arms. The man with the scar looked around and smiled bemusedly, putting his hand up too.

'It has been an honour to live with you all these past months, and it would be an honour to gain shaheedi by your side.'

Raj saw Mehtab smile for the first time, his wild beard and clothes contrasting with an almost gentleness in his eyes.

'We must plan.'

'We should raid that fort near Lahore again,' said Resham Singh. 'We will need supplies if we are to travel.'

'Get a plan together with Vikram Singh and present it to all of us after Rehras Sahib tonight,' ordered Mehtab. Resham clasped his hands together in obedience, giving Vikram a wink.

The group all seemed to have set tasks because as soon as Mehtab dismissed the gathering, they all walked purposefully towards various activities. Most of the men were engaged in looking for firewood, some women were washing clothes, and more men and women were brewing lentils for dinner. Vikram and Resham remained in the tent, drawing things with long wooden twigs into a sandy pit in the corner and whispering quietly to each other.

'So … these guys are clearly going on a suicide mission.' Said Raj quietly to Roop. They were leaning against a thick tree trunk, some metres away from the main site.

'Shaheedi mission,' Roop corrected. 'It does appear so. I can't believe this is happening.'

'I know … you don't think they're planning to take us with them?'

'I don't think Mehtab is going to let us out of his sight. Which doesn't matter anyway; we just need to keep a lookout for the falcon that will take us home.'

Raj could tell Roop was trying to sound surer than she felt; she looked away, deeper into the trees.

'I can't believe how freely they talk about dying,' she said after a while.

'Are you thinking about your mum?'

'About how I would have done and would still do anything to keep her alive and with me. I can't imagine finding anything more important than this life.'

'It's all the legends we read about. Right in front of us- and all I feel is …'

'Guilt?' said Roop. 'Me too. And awe. And also just … look how human they are – washing their clothes, eating *dhaal*, laughing and joking ... they're just like us except ...'

'Except not,' finished Raj. He looked down at his *kara* and felt foolish for wearing it all of a sudden.

'Raj Singh!'

Raj jumped at Vikram's roar. He was standing at the tent entrance, holding a flap open. 'Come here; I need your help with something.'

'Do you see this?' asked Vikram once Raj had joined them in the tent. Resham had drawn a rough sketch of a large square in the sand with the long, pointed wooden stick.

'This is a map of the Mughal fort on the outskirts of Lahore, about half a night of riding away.'

Resham pointed at the edges of the square with his stick. 'These are the outskirts of the fort, and in the centre is their main supply tent. The idea is for half of us to create a distraction on the southern perimeter; the others will then take out the guards stationed at the northern entrance and make their way to the supply tent, load up the horses, and ride like the wind.'

Raj wondered why they were telling him this.

'Er, okay. Did you need any help?'

Resham and Vikram looked at each other. 'We thought you would want to ride with us, surely?'

Raj felt like the ground had been pulled from under his feet. He cleared his throat to make it sound deeper. 'I thought Mehtab Singh had said–'

'We told him you may as well make yourself useful.'

'Oh, thanks.'

'You will be with the team at Northern entrance – under Resham Singh's command. I'll be creating a distraction – setting off some arrows. When you hear my signal, you move through the campsite. It's full of soldiers, so keep your weapons close.'

Raj swallowed, gripping his ornate *kirpan* tightly. He had never actually expected to use it.

Vikram looked at the *kirpan* through Raj's shirt. 'Hey! That's weird; that looks exactly like mine.'

Vikram pulled at his fraying gatra and held up a *kirpan* that looked like a shinier version of Raj's antique one. Raj held back a gasp of surprise; it was the same sword!

'And the guy who made this for me told me it was a one-off design, what a liar!' said Vikram cheerfully, tucking his own *kirpan* out of sight.

Raj thought about the stars in the sky and the *kirpan* hanging around his neck.

It was agreed that six of them would go to the Lahore campsite the following night. Resham, Raj, and Mehtab would be heading to the southern border. Raj groaned when he realised Mehtab would be riding with them.

'He's going to know I'm not from around here as soon as he sees me trying to fight.'

'Well, let's hope it doesn't come to that!' said Roop, helping him try on a battered iron shield to his back. 'The distraction should clear out the soldiers for long enough, and the others will be sleeping.'

'I know you're trying to stop yourself from saying it. Just get it out of your system, come on,' said Raj.

Roop raised her eyebrows innocently, 'Say what?'

A moment passed, and she laughed.

'Okay- maybe you should have stuck out the gatka martial arts lessons at the Gurdwara.'

'I can't believe this. I should just tell them that you're a better fighter than I am–' he said.

'I can't believe I'm not allowed to come,' said Roop, rolling her eyes.

Mehtab had earlier decreed that the women should stay behind and protect the rest of the supplies and horses.

'Roop, if something happens …'

'It won't. It's going to be fine! At least this means they trust us a bit more. Don't go without me – if you find the *Baaj*.'

'What if we can't find a falcon, or we find one, and it doesn't work? Do you think we could stay here forever?'

'I have to believe that we were sent here for a reason. To learn some kind of lesson – there has to be a way back to our lives after that.'

'Raj Singh! Tomorrow we will go and get the raaj!' Vikram Singh shouted, laughing at his own play on Raj's name.

Raj looked back at Roop and saw she was smiling nervously.

'Be brave.'

When he told the Singhs he didn't know how to ride a horse, Vikram and Resham laughed while Mehtab just stared at him, raising one eyebrow.

'What kind of grown man doesn't know how to ride a horse?' asked one of the other elder Singhs joining them on this mission, Kashmir Singh. He was one of the tallest people Raj had ever seen, with long, graceful limbs. He taught him the basics, and Raj felt clumsy and child-like next to him.

'Just keep your back straight; every time you want to go faster, lean forward and squeeze your thighs. When you want to stop, you do the opposite. *Bijali* is the best-behaved horse and my favourite, so you'll answer to me if she gets hurt.'

Raj wasn't sure if he was joking, so he just nodded.

'How do you get around if you don't know how to ride a horse?' asked Kashmir curiously.

'I had an accident when I was younger, so my mum just kept me away from them. Never had much reason to leave my village.'

He didn't sound very convincing; Mehtab was watching them from a few metres away, the light was rapidly fading, and the fire was casting shadows all over his face.

'Don't forget what I said. I have my eye on you,' whispered Mehtab, although somehow still loud enough for Raj to hear.

Kashmir Singh smiled. 'You're in good hands being in Mehtab's jatha. He's the bravest person I know.'

'Why does he hate me so much?'

'He doesn't; his nature is to distrust. He lost his younger brother a few weeks ago. He's been surlier than usual.'

Raj felt a visceral pain explode in his chest. 'Younger brother?'

'Yes, he can't have been more than your age. Mehtab blames himself as it was a random altercation with two soldiers. They shot five arrows through his brother, Mehtab himself barely escaped with his life.'

Raj thought about Bhagat, holding his small body at the hospital when the nurses had told him that some injuries could not be fixed.

CHAPTER SIX

A Breaking of the Dawn

Raj couldn't sleep. The ground was only a few degrees above freezing and the packed earth stone hard. The thin blanket one of the women had given him earlier did almost nothing against the biting night wind, which whistled through the trees all around him. Some Sikhs slept inside the makeshift tents while Roop had managed to secure a spot with some of the other women, but most of the Singhs were braving the cold, so his pride had made him join them. He regretted it now. He had to be the only one left tossing and turning; the others lay still in a neat row next to him, their shapes illuminated by the almost full moon shining from the clear sky.

He gazed up at the stars for a little while longer until his back couldn't take anymore. He wrapped the blanket around his shivering body and felt the ground next to his sleeping mat for his trainers. He reached into his pocket on autopilot for his phone, his go-to when insomnia kicked in back home. Sometimes he would lose track of time, thinking he had spent only a few minutes scrolling social media feeds, when in reality, hours had passed. The phone light would eventually exhaust his eyes enough to make him sleep, but that wasn't an option out here. His phone was now buried at the foot of a wide, green-leafed oak a few metres from the campsite.

He walked along the edge of the clearing, reaching out to touch the tree trunks to guide him; twice he almost tripped on the thick roots, which erupted every so often from the ground. He didn't really know what he was doing, just that he needed to keep moving to stay warm.

He closed his eyes for a second, leaning against a thick trunk.

'What on Earth do you think you're doing?'

Raj knew who the growl belonged to before he had even opened his eyes. Mehtab looked fierce, even in the dim moonlight.

'I couldn't sleep, so I just went for a walk–' began Raj.

'A walk!? I could have killed you if I hadn't recognised you at the last second–'

'Raj?' came Roop's voice from behind Mehtab.

Mehtab whipped around. 'Why are you awake?!'

'I couldn't sleep either …' said Roop. 'I didn't know it was against the rules!'

'I'm freezing,' said Raj. 'I can't feel my fingers.'

'And I'm so hungry I could cry,' added Roop miserably.

Mehtab looked at each of them and then up at the sky as though asking for divine strength or patience.

'Get in that tent,' he said, gesturing to a small, heavily patched tent a few metres away. 'It's the night-guard tent, and I'm on duty tonight.'

They ducked into the shelter gratefully. Inside, a small candle was burning, the cotton wick suspended in what Raj assumed was ghee. It reminded him of the divas his mother used to light all around the house, back when they still celebrated Diwali.

Mehtab closed the tent flaps behind them to block out the cool wind. The tent was sparse, a few blankets piled on a rough sleeping mat, and next to the mat were a set of prayer beads and a long, sheathed iron blade.

Mehtab turned to them.

'Tomorrow is an important mission. I need you to be prepared. Can you fight?' he asked.

'Erm, not really ...' said Raj.

Mehtab crossed his arms over his wide chest and narrowed his eyes as though thinking carefully about something.

'You can't fight, and you can't ride a horse. How have you survived your twenty years?'

'Erm–'

'And what about you?' asked Mehtab, cutting off Raj and turning to Roop.

'I can fight a little bit ...' she said carefully. 'I was taught by our father, but my brother was always frail– poor health ...'

Raj rolled his eyes, vowing to get her back for that later.

'Well, tomorrow he may come face to face with the enemy, and he will need to be ready. Wait here.'

He left the tent.

'Frail?!' said Raj, rounding on Roop, 'Seriously?!'

'I had to make the story realistic! If you had stuck with gatka–'

'Oh we've already had this conversation! Where do you think he's gone?'

Roop looked at the tent entrance nervously. 'It's the middle of the night; surely we're not going to–'

'We're going to train,' said Mehtab, ducking back into the tent, holding a pair of long, wooden sticks. 'Follow me outside.'

'But there's no light–'

'Better to practise in the dark; we're targeting the enemy fort at night.'

'But–'

Mehtab had already left the tent. They looked at each other and then resignedly followed him.

Outside, dawn had begun to break, casting an ethereal, golden glow over the clearing in the forest that Mehtab had led them to. He threw a stick at Roop, who managed to catch it by the very tips of her fingers; it was almost the same size as her.

'Now stand here, get ready.'

Roop took up her position in the clearing. Mehtab charged without warning with his own stick, and Roop pivoted at the very last minute, raising her stick to block.

Raj flinched at the cracking sound of the two sticks colliding. Overhead, a startled bird took flight in alarm.

Roop smiled happily at her quick block, but Mehtab had already turned on his heel, performing a complicated-looking manoeuvre, which ended up with him smacking the wooden stick right on Roop's left ankle.

'Ouch!'

'That's for getting arrogant, get in position again–'

On and on they went until Raj lost track of how many times Roop successfully landed a hit on Mehtab or the greater number of times she ended up falling on her back. Mehtab was ferocious. He seemed to anticipate every move Roop made before she even stepped out of her stance. Raj was beginning to feel sleepy; he sat down, leaning against a trunk. The soft sunlight filtered through the trees, warming his frozen face pleasantly.

'Raj Singh!'

He opened his eyes to see them both looking at him expectantly. He got up on his feet with reluctance, exchanging places with Roop. He gripped the wooden stick carefully, trying to summon some memory of the gatka lessons he had attended regularly until he had lost interest.

Mehtab advanced, and Raj edged backwards until Mehtab shouted at him to stop running and fight. He lifted the stick, but Mehtab had already swung–

'Ow!' Raj yelled, rubbing his shin and then losing balance and falling to the ground. 'You didn't need to actually hit me!'

He got back to his feet, and the same thing happened again.

'I'm not a warrior –I've been trying to tell you–' spluttered Raj as he got back to his feet for the umpteenth time.

'You're not trying,' growled Mehtab. 'You've already decided that you're not good at it, and you're not even trying to change that.'

Raj opened his mouth to protest, but Mehtab had already charged at him again with the stick; he stopped right at Raj's throat.

'Now my right side is completely exposed, land your blow there. Do it!' instructed Mehtab.

It felt like many days had passed before Mehtab finally listened to Raj and Roop's joint pleas to allow them a break before they passed out with exhaustion. Mehtab permitted them to return to the campsite to collect water from a large urn kept near the firepit. Afterwards, he told them to join him in the guard tent again. Raj could barely keep his eyes open.

'You're reckless,' said Mehtab to Roop as they entered the tent again. He looked over at Raj before adding, 'And you don't even seem to want to survive.'

Mehtab sat down, cross-legged.

'I don't know where you have come from, and no matter what the others say, there's still something I don't trust about you. You're both distracted; your thoughts are elsewhere – with people who are not here anymore.'

Raj glanced at Roop, but they both said nothing.

'The battle is won or lost in the mind before ever being fought on the battlefield. All the best soldiers in history have understood this. I've fought many ferocious enemies, but none as powerful as my own mind.'

There was silence.

'I was thinking about my mum,' admitted Roop quietly after a few minutes had passed. 'I miss her.'

'Your sensitivity to the cold, to hunger, to the highs and lows of the world, they all come from a lack of control over the mind. Direct your attention to something else, to something bigger than us, the potential that lives inside all of us. That only comes through meditation. Sit down and close your eyes.'

Roop met Raj's eye and raised her eyebrow.

'Now!'

They both jumped and hurriedly fell to their knees, crossing their aching legs.

'Clear your mind, let the silence all around you in,' instructed Mehtab.

Raj squeezed his eyes shut, and all he could think about was the cold, the hunger, the sore throbbing on his ankles and knees where Mehtab had hit him – and fear. Then a few minutes later, all he could see was Bhagat. He tried to say 'Waheguru' the way he could hear Roop muttering under her breath next to him, but the memories played out in front of him like a movie. He was picking at the wound of grief, and he knew it, yet he couldn't seem to stop. He gave a frustrated sigh and opened his eyes again.

'I'm not doing that,' he said resolutely. 'It doesn't work for me. All I keep thinking about is my – our – brother.'

Mehtab opened just one of his eyes, and his hand continued to move on his mala.

Roop opened her eyes next to him. 'And I keep thinking about mum.'

Mehtab's expression was unreadable; he had opened both eyes now and was watching them both intently. The silence stretched out all around them.

'As long as you maintain your sense of separation from the Creator, the more you will suffer. Your attachment is a chain around your chest,' Mehtab said finally.

Roop cleared her throat. 'With all due respect, we're suffering because we lost people that we really loved. How are we not supposed to be attached to the people we love? We can't all be like you – all of you here, brave and unaffected and unattached – no matter how much we might try –'

'My brother died in my arms. While we were on a mission. He was young – hadn't even married yet. One minute we were riding the forests that we knew like the back of our hands, and the next he had more arrows in his chest than I could count,' said Mehtab, matter of factly.

'I didn't know –' began Roop.

'We know love. It's the only reason we are here. And you don't think that we feel fear? That the constant living under the threat of death doesn't take its toll? The courage you see in us is not the absence of fear; it is kept alive by a small and simple belief that other things are more important.'

'But it's all well when you say that,' continued Roop bravely, 'but all I think about, constantly, is her – there's no space for anything else. How do I get rid of that?'

Raj had never heard Roop talk so freely about her emotions. She was looking determinedly at Mehtab as though yearning for an answer.

'You close your eyes, and you focus. Stop running away from the thoughts that are haunting you, accept them – lean into them, so you can hear what they have to say, and then turn your attention to something else. Decide that there are more things to live for than to break for. The battle is won or lost in the mind before it is ever fought on the field.'

Raj closed his eyes again, and the tent fell quiet. Bhagat's face rose, unbidden, in his mind again. Bhagat sitting at the kitchen table doing his homework, Bhagat begging him for a go on his game console, Bhagat trying to negotiate his way out of chores, Bhagat making everyone laugh, Bhagat dropping his school bag in the living room to watch cartoons, a car accident, the end of the world, a numbness settling on Raj's brain, a suffocating vice around his chest as he gazed around Bhagat's bedroom, which now belonged to a dead child – a dead child, the worst sentence in the world, it floated around his mind's eye. Raj gasped, but he kept his eyes shut, leaned into the grief, and it was like running down a tunnel of darkness, begging for light which you had been promised but had never seen. He whispered 'Waheguru' over and over, and slowly the vice around his chest had slackened; he let out a long breath he hadn't realised he was holding.

When he opened his eyes, Mehtab was no longer there, and the light of dawn had begun to break all around the tent, dispelling the darkness of the preceding night.

CHAPTER SEVEN

The First Mission

The next day was spent in preparation for the mission. While the other Sikhs helped sharpen swords, feed horses, and rehearse the plan, Raj and Roop were given duties to wash the clothes and help prepare more dhaal and roti for breakfast. The food was carefully portioned. When Raj felt in the iron drum for ground flour to make into dough, he found the supply almost depleted. Raj drank his dhaal like he had yesterday and wondered how the meal had made him even more hungry than he'd been before he had it. He looked around at the others, none of them complained, but he watched the way they wiped the very last bit of dhaal from the iron bowls with their thin rotis and scraped their plates for any crumbs of roti before adding them to the basket of dishes to wash. Raj wondered for the hundredth time how they had managed to survive for this long.

Raj managed to escape Mehtab's watchful eye and take a short nap behind the langat tent at lunchtime. He had managed to fall into an exhausted slumber before being elbowed awake by Roop, who urged him to practise some more fighting before the mission started.

They finally set off in what felt like the darkest part of the night after doing a short ardas, led by Mehtab. The forest around them was impenetrably silent apart from the sounds of creaking branches and rustling leaves. Bijali seemed to know to follow the others intuitively and could see better than Raj in the dark. They rode together for what felt like a few hours. The basic training Kashmir Singh had given him had Raj exercising some control over the horse, but after some time, the pain in his lower back became searing, sending waves up his whole back, all the way to the base of his skull. He knew he couldn't ask for a break, though, as the timings had been carefully planned.

After what felt like an eternity riding the uneven ground between tall trees, they reached a clearing in the forest, where a fallen tree lay on its side. Raj took a deep breath, relieved at finally reaching open space.

'This is where we split up,' said Mehtab breaking the silence softly, the almost-full moon illuminating his wild beard. They said Fateh to each other, and Vikram, Kashmir, and the Singh with a long scar on his face headed left through the trees towards the Southern perimeter of the Lahore fort.

Raj, Mehtab, and Resham turned right into what felt like an even denser part of the jungle. He soon lost sense of time again, the jolts of pain in his back becoming rhythmically aligned to the cantering pace of the horses; even the soft sounds of the horses breathing became hypnotic. Twice he became overcome with fatigue and almost slid off his horse; Resham pushed him gently back each time, urging him awake.

When Mehtab finally stopped and jumped down from his horse, Raj found that he couldn't move at all. His legs and back had become frozen in the night air, the pain in his back now almost unbearable. He felt Resham grip his arm.

'No,' said Mehtab, in the darkness. 'He can come down on his own.'

'I can't–'

'Move your toes first, then your ankle, and work your way up. Then slide gently off the side of the horse,' Mehtab instructed.

Raj did as he was told and felt the pain become steadily more pronounced until he felt like he would cry aloud in agony. He slid slowly off the side of the horse, slipping and landing face down in the muddy floor of the clearing

He felt arms gripping him and pulling him straight and was surprised when he realised it was Mehtab.

'A soldier needs to be able to carry his own weight in battle, Raj Singh.'

'What about when he can't?' said Raj, feeling his legs shake under him.

Mehtab gripped his shoulder tightly. 'The battle is won or lost in the mind before it is ever fought on the field.'

They tied the horses around the thickest trunks in the clearing and continued on foot, Resham tapping a tree here and there as they went, as some kind of navigation method. As his muscles loosened, Raj leaned off Mehtab, muttering a thanks, which was ignored.

The light of the moon became steadily stronger as the trees dwindled. Mehtab eventually held up his hand for them to stop, and they tucked themselves behind an ancient-looking oak tree. Raj peeked around the edge of the gnarled and twisted trunk; he could make out a rough, clay-brick structure. It looked hastily built but well-guarded. He could see lights moving around inside, even from a distance.

'Now we wait for the signal from Vikram's jatha. Once we are inside the compound, follow my lead straight to the supply tent in the centre.'

'And there won't be any guards along the way?'

'We will move stealthily and quietly – no violence unless we are provoked.'

'And what if we are provoked?' he asked.

'Then make your strike sure and true; send the Turks on to answer for their crimes in the true king's court.'

Raj was hit with a wave of dizziness, which made the dark landscape spin dangerously in front of him, and his legs trembled again as though they were going to give way. He tried to slide down the trunk to sit at the tree's base, but Mehtab hissed at him to get up and into warrior stance. Raj had no idea what that was, but he copied Resham's half-crouch and listened hard to the darkness around them.

And then suddenly, there was a sound of a conch-shell, which Raj recognised from the campsite when the Singhs had been practising, and then the fort really came to life. Fire lanterns were immediately lit along the edge of the structure to respond to the threat. They could hear a long rumble, the sound of the gate on the other side of the fort opening, and then a few minutes later, came the sound of hundreds of hoofs. Mehtab gestured for them to wait and then nodded. They sprinted the last few metres of forest and then into the exposed clearing leading to the gates of the fort, the most dangerous part of their journey so far. Raj didn't look up or left or right; he kept his head down, watched his feet moving faster than they ever had before. They flattened themselves against the clay walls, Raj breathing much harder than the other two.

Resham crawled on his stomach to the base of the gate and then pulled out a special powder from the pocket of his fraying *chola*. It created a brief spark, and then he was burning a hole into the corner of the wooden gate. Resham hastily put out the sparks once the hole was the right size. They crawled through one by one and finally into the fort.

As they had planned, no guards were standing immediately in front of this gate, their attention now being focussed firmly on the southern side. The courtyard in front of them was square, with doors and curtains hung around at intervals along the edges, leading to further rooms. In the middle, some metres away, was a large tent. They looked at each other; Mehtab nodded once, and they crept cautiously towards it - but there were no guards anywhere to be seen. Raj felt discomfited. Surely they wouldn't have left their supplies totally abandoned in this way? The Sikhs had left their modest grains with a full guard – and even Raj understood that in this world, your supplies were not easily replenished and could be the difference between victory and defeat, life, and death.

The flap to the tent was half-open; Resham peeked in, grabbing a lantern from a socket in the wall near them.

'It's clear.'

They followed him inside; Raj had been expecting more – but Vikram and Mehtab both smiled at each other. The space was small, taken up by several open brown sacks of flour, more white sacks filled to the brim with lentils, and a single, small bag of what looked like salt and one of sugar. At the very back of the tent, there were a few cages of sleeping livestock. With Resham's lamp, he could make out a few sleeping chickens – and – a *baaj*!

'Mehtab Singh – look, it's a *baaj*!' exclaimed Raj.

'Raj, grab that sack of flour and take it to the front. Come back for the *dhaal,*' responded Mehtab without looking up.

Raj felt a growing sense of elation – maybe this ordeal would soon finally be over. He almost hugged Mehtab but restrained himself. They created a line to the gate, passing down a few sacks of flour and *dhaal* to the entrance.

'Right, let's get out of here.' said Mehtab, pocketing the bag of sugar, the tent now empty apart from the cages at the back.

'I just need to get the *Baaj* –'

'Don't be stupid. We can't eat a *Baaj*,' said Resham.

'But-'

'HEY! STOP RIGHT THERE! SIKHS IN THE FORT! SIKHS IN THE FORT!'

Raj looked up, on the second floor of the fort, at a lookout post, a single Turk soldier was pointing his sword at them.

'Come down here and fight us like a man!' roared Mehtab. As Resham released a dagger tucked away near his shoe, it met the Turk's neck, and he fell from his post, landing with a sickening crunch near Raj's feet. Raj tried not to look at the blood now pooling around his feet, but his vision blurred all the same.

'Get a move on!' yelled Mehtab, pushing him towards the gate. They raced towards the fort gate, the sound of hooves now louder than ever as the army returned from dealing with Vikram's distraction. As they reached the entrance, Raj felt the sickening sensation grow – he was so close to their escape route from this time period. There was no way he could walk away from it; he had to go back. He turned around and began running back to the tent, ignoring Mehtab's roar and Resham's shout of warning. Just as he reached the flap of the tent, he was gripped like a vice from behind, his throat caught in a sweaty arm with a force strong enough to lift him off his feet.

'You thought you were clever? You will regret the day you thought you could cross us,' whispered a foul-smelling, accented voice in his ear.

'We've got the other one!' yelled another voice behind them. The soldier spun Raj around to see Mehtab, restrained by three soldiers, being marched back to the courtyard.

'You stupid idiot!' yelled Mehtab. 'I knew you were going to get us killed!'

Raj realised with a sinking certainty that Mehtab must have stayed back for him. Suddenly, a strike of lightning lit up the darkness around them; the guards shouted in shock, and Mehtab took advantage of the momentary distraction to break free. He pulled a short *kirpan* from the back of his boot and took out the guards nearest to him, he threw another knife at the big guard behind Raj's back, and the man let out a blood-curdling scream, his grip immediately slackening. Raj ran as fast as he could towards Mehtab.

'Get back to camp and tell them to go. They'll be searching the forests after this,' ordered Mehtab.

Raj could make out shouts and the sound of more soldiers running towards them. The sky roared with thunder, and rain began to fall.

'Come with me!' shouted Raj.

'I'm not running away from a fight,' growled Mehtab. 'Get out of here, now!'

Raj wanted to protest, but his feet were carrying him towards the fort entrance before he knew it. The night and the rain enveloped him like a blanket of invisibility, and he ran.

As Raj wandered through the darkness, his memory of the accident that killed Bhagat came to the forefront of his mind. It was incomplete and hazy. There was an impact, lots of pain, shock, the light of ambulances, the sounds of random passers-by trying to comfort him, the feeling of someone – maybe a paramedic gripping him very hard by the shoulders. The only thing he could remember clearly – too clearly in fact – was the way his mother's face had dropped when she arrived in the hospital to find him waiting in the corridor outside the intensive care unit. He realised then they hadn't told her which son would be OK and which one was fighting for his life. She had broken down, started the beginnings of several prayers, began banging on the glass of the door until an exhausted-looking junior doctor came out to ask her to stop. She hadn't looked at Raj. She didn't look at dad either when he was eventually released to join them. Raj knew he was supposed to try and comfort them – he was the eldest son – he was supposed to be helping to hold them together. Instead, he barged open the double door of the unit and ran, and ran, and ran.

He wandered around the dark forest for most of the night, but eventually, exhaustion kicked in, and now he was staggering through the darkness, gripping low-hanging branches for support. His body was covered in bruises and cuts, an open wound on his hand was dripping blood. The rain had stopped, but he was soaking wet. The cotton material of the borrowed tunic sticking to him like a second skin. He had no idea where he was or where he was going. All he could see in his head was Mehtab's fierce eyes, and then Bhagat's steady brown ones, and him running each time. It was all his fault – he had got the leader of the jatha captured and almost certainly killed; what would the other Sikhs do now? What if they all got captured? What if Roop was dead?

Raj felt nausea rising from his gut, and he retched multiple times at the base of the nearest tree. It was the first time he had stopped moving for hours, and he swayed a little on his feet. He felt bone-tired, like he couldn't carry on even one more step. He collapsed onto the wet forest floor and drifted away into the darkness.

He awoke to the feeling of warm light on his face. When he opened his eyes, he blinked furiously, trying to adjust to the brightness after hours in the dark. It took a few minutes to remember yesterday's events. What was he supposed to do now? He needed to find his way back to Roop – she must think he was dead – and then … then what? Maybe she would be better off without him anyway. He had got her into this whole mess, and Mehtab was going to be killed, and …

He forced himself to take a deep breath, and without realising it, he was praying. He hadn't prayed like this before. He closed his eyes, pressing his eyeballs deeper into his skull with his palms. He didn't know how long he was there, but suddenly the sound of a horse brought him back to the present. He leapt up behind the tree trunk, his heart racing like a wild animal.

'Come out. I know you're there!' It was a woman's voice. Raj peeked around the tree. A woman got down from the back of a white horse. She wore a long, blue tunic with light coloured bottoms. Multiple swords hung from her body, and a battered shield was tied loosely to the horse's saddle.

'I'm a Sikh,' she said, 'you don't need to be scared of me.'

She put a light-coloured scarf over her head and pulled a shawl tighter to her body.

'Come on. I don't have all day.'

Raj hesitated. What choice did he have? He couldn't hide in the forest for much longer with no food or water and no way of getting back home.

'There he is.' She looked him up and down as he staggered out from behind the tree, and Raj felt shy all of a sudden. She couldn't have been much older than him. 'I wanted to see who was brave enough to steal from the Lahore fort.'

'I'm not brave,' he said quickly. 'I didn't do anything.'

She put her hands on her hips and studied him for a few seconds. 'Where's Mehtab Singh?'

He felt a deep pit of shame open in his stomach. 'He got captured – he told me to go. I did try to stay, but he said I should run and warn the others–'

She let out a low whistle. 'So the rumours are true. The Jathedar has been captured.'

'It was my fault,' he said miserably, kicking the tree trunk with his battered trainers. 'He came back to try and save me.'

'That sounds like Mehtab,' she said. 'Here.'

She handed him a rough, canvas canteen of water. When he raised it to his lips, he felt he had never tasted anything sweeter.

'Better?'

He nodded, handing it back to her. She slung it over a shoulder. She looked weather-beaten, her skin tanned and lined. A long, thin scar ran down one side of her face.

'You can stop staring at it. You'll likely have one of your own anyway.' She moved closer to touch his face. 'We need to get that looked at.'

He hadn't even realised there were thin rivulets of blood dripping down onto his T-shirt. He pulled back, turning away from her.

'I'll take you back to the others. I know their location,' she called after him.

'How would you know that? Who are you?' he asked, turning back to her.

'My name is Jeet Kaur. I know most things about this forest – it is my home. Now get on the horse; I don't have all day.'

'I'm not sure I want to go back to the jatha.'

She raised her eyebrow. 'So you plan to wander around the forests on your own until you die? They'll be scouring these forests, you know. It won't take long for the Turks to find you at all – you're rubbish at covering your tracks.'

'I'm the reason Mehtab is captured – probably dead. Why would they want to see me? I'm a coward.'

'The only cowardly thing to do would be not to go back. Mehtab told you to warn the others, remember?'

She watched him with that piercing gaze for a little longer, and Raj squirmed uncomfortably. There was something about her that reminded him of Roop. Maybe that was why he clambered up onto her horse behind her, and then they were charging through the forest. At some point, his head fell onto the back of her shoulder, into a restless slumber.

69

CHAPTER EIGHT

Escape to the Safehouse

When Raj opened his eyes again, he was suspended once again in that pitch-black darkness.

'Jeet?' he called quietly, feeling the ground around him. He knew they were now inside, but he hadn't been inside a proper building since they had left Oxford. Could it be that he had dreamed up the whole experience? He would definitely be going to see his GP about his meds …

'Quiet!' came Jeet's voice from near him, shattering Raj's desperate hope.

'Where are we?' he whispered back. 'Where are you?'

Her voice seemed to be coming from everywhere; his eyes had begun to adjust, and he could make out hazy outlines of furniture in the room.

'I had to ride us out of the forest, too many Turks everywhere.'

He felt the tight fear closing around his chest again, like a vice. 'Do you think the others will be okay? We were supposed to go back and warn them, Mehtab told me to –'

Jeet shushed him again. 'We can talk about this in the morning.'

'Can you tell me where we are?!'

'I can't believe you slept during the most crucial hours of our ride, and now when being unconscious would actually be really helpful, you're awake!'

'Why didn't you wake me up? If we were in trouble?'

She snorted. 'We weren't in any trouble – I could handle a couple of Turk search parties in my sleep. But you're in no shape to fight.' She hesitated as though it pained her to admit it. 'Maybe I just felt sorry for you.'

Raj's head was throbbing, his wound had stopped bleeding, but his whole arm felt heavy, as though he was dragging around the weight of someone else's limb.

'Are you going to tell me where we are?' he asked again.

'Is it so difficult to whisper?' she hissed.

Raj sighed in exasperation.

'We're at a safe house – a small settlement near the village. I've known this family for years; they always let me stay here when there is an emergency,' she said finally.

'But isn't that really dangerous for them?'

'Obviously. That's why I'm telling you to shut up and sleep. If soldiers find us here, we're not the only ones getting killed.'

'But why would they take that risk?' asked Raj quietly, 'what do they get out of it?'

'You're more cynical than I am,' Jeet replied. 'Sometimes, there's no reason for doing things. You just do it because you think it's the right thing to do.'

'Are they Sikhs?'

'They love Guru Nanak. Probably more than you and I – to be hiding his Khalsa in their house, on pain of death.'

She yawned, then quickly stifled it. 'Get some rest. We'll set out in a couple of hours back to the campsite. They should have given up by then.'

'What if they've found them …' said Raj, trailing off, unable to finish his thought.

'Don't underestimate them, Raj. Anyway, no point in worrying about things that haven't happened yet. You'll go mad.'

Raj was quiet, he heard Jeet's breaths get longer and deeper, and eventually, he fell asleep too.

'I've never seen him before –'

'He looks very young –'

'He's bleeding badly, Rano – go and get some water and bandages.'

Raj heard the low voices around him and willed his eyes open. The room was now lit in a dim, dawn light, filtering through the open door a few metres away from him. Surrounded by concerned-looking faces, he reached for his kirpan, shuffling away from them until the oldest man – with short white hair and a short beard held up his hands and smiled kindly.

'We're not going to hurt you, Son. We're Jeet's friends.'

Raj looked around at the other faces; there was an older woman who he guessed was the man's wife, and a younger man, who had the same dark, almond-shaped eyes and closely cut white hair, though his had more specks of brown. Two children stood near the door, a boy and girl; they were smiling at him shyly, nudging each other as though daring one another to get closer.

Raj sat up from the floor he had been sleeping on, pulling away a woollen blanket that someone must have draped on him overnight. The room was small and clearly ordinarily used as some kind of storage space, with large sacks and wooden drums lining the walls around him.

'Where's Jeet?' he asked nervously.

'She is tending to her horse herself,' replied the younger man. 'Never lets any of us do it.'

Another woman came through the door, holding a wide, iron bowl filled with water and some pieces of white linen.

'My wife will clean your wounds,' said the younger man. 'My name is Arjun. And this is my older brother Heera.'

Raj hesitated as the woman got closer. 'I can do it.'

'She's very good,' replied Arjun. 'The best in our village at healing.'

The woman wasn't making eye contact with him; she pulled her rough brown shawl closer to her body and then knelt beside him, dipping a cloth into the water. She dabbed his face gently as Raj closed his eyes and vowed never to take cleanliness for granted again.

'Thank you,' he said, clearing his throat. 'You have saved our lives.'

Heera nodded sagely. 'These are troubled times.'

The older woman that Raj assumed was Heera's wife put a hand on his shoulder. 'We should go and get some food.'

Raj's stomach gave a loud rumble at the sound of food, and the woman smiled at him fondly before leading Heera from the room.

Rano had finished cleaning his face and was now cleaning the cuts on his hands and arm.

'Are those your children?' asked Raj, gesturing to the boy and girl still smiling at him from the doorway.

Arjun laughed, waving them in. 'Come inside. Don't be scared – he's not going to hurt you.'

'But he's got a *kirpan*!' said the boy.

'Can I see it?' asked the girl eagerly, coming into the room.

'Sorry,' said Arjun, 'they've never seen a Singh up close before. Normally it's only Jeet that stays here.'

Raj smiled, his face muscles aching as though he had forgotten how to do that. He showed them the peacock *kirpan,* and the boy traced the pattern on the hilt with awe.

'That's the best one I've ever seen,' he said happily. 'When's the last time you used it?!'

Raj stopped smiling and tucked the *kirpan* back under his dirty shirt.

'I haven't used it. I'm not that good at fighting.'

'But you're a khalsa! How can you not be good at fighting?' asked the girl, raising her eyebrow.

The sight of Mehtab and his wild eyes, twirling daggers in his hands, flashed in Raj's mind.

'That's enough,' interjected Arjun. 'Go and find some clean clothes. Ask your Thaiyee.'

They left the room obediently.

Rano unrolled the linen and began to tie his arm tight. He let out a hiss.

'Sorry,' she said quietly. 'You are in a lot of pain.'

'It's OK. It's just a flesh wound really –'

'I wasn't talking about your wounds,' she said in the same quiet voice. She looked up at him and then tapped his forehead softly. 'I meant in there.'

Raj looked at Arjun for some kind of explanation, but he just shrugged. 'She's the best in the village,' he said again.

'I don't have a headache –' Raj said.

She smiled. 'You know what I'm talking about. Even if you don't want to admit it. You have wounds inside your mind and soul, which you haven't healed. You won't get to where you need to unless you do.'

'Where do I need to go?'

'You're trying to get back home, but home is far away. You're heartbroken. You've lost someone you love.'

Raj felt his throat constrict. 'I lost my brother.'

She nodded sympathetically. 'You lost yourself too.'

Arjun cleared his throat. 'Rano, that's enough. Sometimes people are not ready to hear these things.'

Rano nodded, going back to her work. Heera came in, carrying a plate laden with more food than Raj had seen in days. He tried to be patient while Rano finished cleaning and dressing the wounds on his face, but his stomach gave a loud rumble – which sounded like an earthquake in the small room. Rano grinned, then quickly suppressed her smile, looking down to wring out the cloth.

'You can laugh,' said Raj. 'I don't mind.'

'I'll let you eat, then finish,' she said kindly.

Raj didn't have it in him to refuse the offer; he dived on the plate. Soft white rotis, thick steaming hot dhaal, cooked gajaran – even some kheer. The food tasted more similar to the kind his mum might make, but it still had a strange, foreign aftertaste to it. It was only after he had mopped up the last of the dhaal with his roti that he thought guilty of Resham, Vikram, and the dozen others, and the way they gazed at their own meals of watery dhaal and dried roti as if they too were eating feasts.

'I haven't eaten like that in a while.' he said, feeling like he needed to explain.

Arjun and Heera looked at each other and smiled.

'I remember eating only sholey daaney for days on end,' said Heera, gazing off into the distance, beyond the room's slightly ajar door.

Raj didn't understand. 'When was that?'

Arjun laid a hand on his elder brother's shoulder. 'You don't need to –'

Heera shook his head. 'No, I want him to know … I used to be in the khalsa too. Had a long flowing beard, tied a blue dumalla, even had a chakar on mine.'

He smiled fondly at his memories, still not making eye contact with anyone in the room.

'But I ran away after only a few months … I'll never forget the look on my father's face when he saw that his eldest son – the one he had said belonged to the Khalsa, came back with a shaved head.'

'It broke his heart,' agreed Arjun sadly, looking down at the floor. 'He never was the same after that.'

'My dad was a devout Sikh, you see. He was in the crowd the day the Khalsa was created at Anandpur Sahib. They had darshan of Sri Guru Gobind Singh Ji themselves.'

Raj felt goosebumps rise on his skin. 'Did they tell you what they looked like?' he asked eagerly. 'Were they like the pictures?'

'What pictures?' asked Heera confusedly.

'Nothing,' said Raj hurriedly. 'Did they meet them?!'

'No, they saw them from afar – we would eagerly ask them in the same way if they remembered what they looked like, but our father would always say that there were no words to describe the radiance of Guru Gobind Singh Jee appropriately. That day, Father was going to be blessed with Amrit, but something was holding him back. Because of that doubt, he didn't take the blessing of pahul. He died a few years ago, but before he went, he said this was our seva now. This was why we didn't have the Khalsa roop, so we could help the Khalsa when it was in need. Serving is our family's purpose now. All the Sikhs know that this is a safe house, a place for them to rest, be fed, be comforted,' responded Heera.

There was a short silence. Rano had picked up the linen again to finish bandaging his wounds. Her hands were gentle.

'Not a day goes by that he doesn't think about the Khalsa,' said Rano, looking up at her brother-in-law. 'But he serves an important purpose here.'

Heera looked at Raj's dastaar with an unreserved longing in his eyes. 'It's a strange thing ... it's been so many years since I left. I've since married ... had children ... worked the farmland in all seasons of the year, yet something about the forest calls me ... no, pulls me. Here.' He gestured to the centre of his chest. 'You are blessed and brave, Raj Singh, to be wearing your father's turban and sword in these times.'

Raj wanted to protest – he hadn't lived with his turban and sword in these times at all; he had spent his twenty years of life in the United Kingdom, taking all these things for granted, feeling mostly apathetic about his Sikh identity.

He opened his mouth to talk, but Heera continued, 'I still do my nitnem, though. They can't take that away from me. I had it memorised, and I was so scared of forgetting it, I repeated it over and over again for days.'

'You don't have a *gutka*- or ...' Raj trailed off, realising his mistake.

Arjun shook his head sadly. 'We can't keep one in the house – in case of surprise raids. People come and go but keeping *gurbani* here all the time would be a big risk.'

Raj thought about all the places where he read *gurbani* every day, even the days he didn't want to – the apps on his phone, the projector screens at Sikh Soc meetings, the whiteboard near the entrance of his local gurdwara. He felt a profound, deep sadness at the idea of that all being taken away.

'But we have taught the children,' said Arjun proudly. 'The *gurbani* keeps us alive – and the seva.'

'Aren't you scared you will be caught helping us all?'

Heera shrugged, bending to pick up the now empty plate in front of Raj. 'Death is coming for all of us; the time and place is already written, nothing we can do to stop it.

His wife came in then, carrying some clean clothes. They left him alone while he wiped down the rest of the dirt using the bowl of water that Rano had left for him and changed.

'You all bandaged up?'

He looked up as Jeet entered the room a few minutes later; she had changed too, into dark, loose-fitting tunic and trousers. He counted three kirpans strapped to her body.

'Yeah,' he replied, lifting his bound arm. 'Are we leaving soon?'

'Did you get creeped out by Rano? She did the same thing to me when I first came here. She knew everything.'

'What is everything?' asked Raj carefully, pulling on his battered trainers.

Jeet shrugged. 'Same thing that has happened to a lot of people – nothing special. The forest is my home now. I grew up there, know everything there is to know about it.'

Just then came the sound of hooves on a stone courtyard. The door to the room swung open, and Arjun motioned for them to get into a large, dark, wooden cupboard in the corner of the room, lifting his fingers to his lips. Jeet seized the back of Raj's shirt, pulling them both into the cramped space. Arjun closed the door on them, and they fell back into darkness. All he could hear was his own breathing. A few inches away from him, Jeet was as silent as a ghost.

'Are they soldiers?'

'No – sounds like bounty hunters to me. Must be from the village.'

Raj gulped. 'Bounty hunters?!'

'Sikh heads fetch a heavy price in these parts.'

Raj pressed his ear against the wood of the door. He could hear two or three male voices, raised and harsh, and the softer, placating tones of Heera and Arjun.

'I think they're coming inside,' he whispered. 'Jeet?'

Jeet didn't respond; he tapped her shape softly. 'Are you OK?'

She flinched. 'I'm fine. They'll go away – just be quiet.'

The voices got louder, Heera and Arjun offering the same repeated reassurances.

'We haven't seen anyone. It's just my family inside – my wife.'

'Bring her out then,' came the response.

'There's no need for disrespecting …' There was the dull sound of a slap, someone hitting the floor.

'Don't answer back to us! We'll have you and your brother in front of the governor. And you know what they'll do to your wives …'

Raj felt explosive anger spreading through his veins as the man continued with a series of coarse and ugly threats. He reached for his *kirpan,* and before he could think about it, he stretched out a hand to push the cupboard door open.

'No,' whispered Jeet finally, grabbing his hand. 'If they find out we are here, everyone is dead.'

'The things he's saying –' Raj spluttered, his fury making it hard for him to get coherent sentences out.

'I know.'

'If he touches any of them – or the kids –'

'It's a hundred times worse for them all if they find us here,' she whispered back.

'I don't care – if I die or whatever – I'm not listening to …'

'They will kill them all, Raj – not just you!'

They heard the door to the room creak open and both fell silent immediately.

'What is this room for?' asked a rough voice.

'This is where we store grain,' said Heera.

Raj had never felt his heart beat this fast before; surely they could hear it outside in the room? The beat seemed to sink deeper into his stomach, fear, anger, and dread pulsing in the whole of his body. A powerful, sickening scent had filled the room – of sweat, blood, dirt.

His hands had found the kirpan again now; he had begun to pull at the hilt when –

'A Sikh! Near the forest! We've found one!'

There was a commotion then, more low threats from the men, which made Raj's skin crawl, and then they barged out of the room, the door slamming behind them. Raj let out a long breath.

'Jeet, are you OK?'

'This isn't the first time this has happened to me,' she began. 'This same situation … only they didn't leave until they found my whole family.'

Raj didn't know what to say; instead, he reached out to grip her forearm, and they stood together, in the dark.

It was a few minutes before the door to the wardrobe was opened again. Rano stood there patiently; her eyes had the same faraway look as before, as though the events of the last half an hour had never happened.

'They've gone,' she said simply.

Raj and Jeet climbed out of the wardrobe. He felt exposed suddenly; the room didn't feel like the safe haven it had just a short while ago. Muddy footsteps covered the floor in the room, the faint smell of the men – of sweat and mud – lingered. Heera came in, a large bruise forming under his eye.

'Your face –' began Raj.

He waved a hand to dismiss their concerns and gestured his wife forward. She came in holding a small bundle.

'This is all the food we could spare, plus some other supplies.'

'You'll need to change your bandages in a few hours,' said Rano softly.

'That was a close call,' said Jeet, pulling a shawl over her body. 'I don't know how to …'

'You know better than to say thank you,' said Heera. 'Arjun is waiting in the courtyard; he's got your horse out of the hiding place.'

'You could all have been killed – and worse – because of us,' said Raj. He couldn't understand how they were all so calm.

Heera came over, placing a heavy hand on Raj's shoulder. 'It's nothing we wouldn't do again, and again, and again.'

Raj swallowed a rise of emotion in his throat. 'It won't always be like this.'

'I think Rano is rubbing off on him; he's also making prophecies,' said Jeet, casting a sideways glance at Raj.

Rano smiled, a faint uplifting of her lips. 'He's not making prophecies. He's seen everything. He is sure.'

Raj looked at her and felt sure that Rano knew exactly where he was from. He had a hundred questions for her but knew there was no time.

'Let's get out of here, and we'll try not to come back … at least for a while,' Jeet added, smiling sheepishly at Heera.

The kids surprised him with hugs as they appeared in a large, tidy courtyard. The sun had risen high in the sky now.

'Shouldn't we wait for it to get dark?' Raj asked nervously, looking around.

'Where's the brave boy who was about to go after a group of fully armed bounty hunters single-handedly back there?' said Jeet, raising an eyebrow.

'Not single-handedly ... I thought you would join me. And that wasn't brave ...'

She shrugged. 'Could have fooled me. Anyway, I'm riding us like the wind out of here while they're still distracted with whatever poor soul has just wandered out of the forest.'

Arjun handed her the reins of her beloved horse and raised a final hand in farewell.

'I'll never forget you.' said Raj quietly to Heera.

He gave Raj a smile and a clap on the back before he and Arjun stepped back to join the rest of their family. Raj climbed the horse behind Jeet, holding tight as they rode fast through the tiny hamlet and back into the trees.

He must have fallen asleep again because when he opened his eyes, it was dark again. He got up, feeling around to try and get a sense of where he was. His hand hit something solid.

'Ouch! Watch it!'

'Roop?! Is that you?'

'Yes – keep your voice down; you're going to wake everyone up.'

'Am I back at the campsite?'

'Yes – Jeet brought you back a few hours ago. You've been totally out of it – you were gibbering random stuff under your breath when they were tending to your wounds.'

He touched the new, thick bandage wrapped around his hand and then his face and felt tears in his eyes. He blinked a few times, feeling grateful for the darkness.

'It was all my fault. I got Mehtab captured, and then we almost got Heera and his family killed.'

'I should have known you would blame yourself, wait – who is Heera?' she asked.

'I ran, Roop, I ran and left Mehtab behind. I should have fought by his side – they've probably executed him by now,' Raj continued, unable to look at her.

'The Sikhs here don't think so,' said Roop softly. 'Vikram and Resham and the others all got back some hours before you did. The Turks won't want to kill Mehtab; he is way too valuable.'

'Valuable? Roop, that just means they'll torture him to get the location of the others. That's even worse!'

'Look, we don't know what's happening, so there's no point speculating. In the morning, we'll figure out some kind of plan …' she responded, putting a comforting hand on his shoulder.

'There's no way we can get back into the Lahore fort now.' said Raj miserably.

'That's very defeatist of you.' a new voice came from the other side of Raj. He jumped closer to Roop, and there was a sound of a match being struck before a small candle illuminated the laughing face of Jeet Kaur. 'Sorry, didn't mean to frighten you.'

'I wasn't frightened,' said Raj, feeling embarrassed. 'We just attacked that fort – there's no way that we'll get a second shot. They will have tightened up their defences.'

'Or maybe precisely because we did just take out the fort, they won't be expecting a second hit. You know the story of Baba Bidhi Chand, right?'

'Of course, but he had the help of Guru Hargobind Sahib Jee. We're just out here on our own.'

Jeet snorted. 'Speak for yourself. Actually …'

She leaned forward, pulling at the gatra around his chest. 'You have some audacity talking about the Guru abandoning you when you wear His *kirpan* every single day.'

Raj squirmed away from her. 'That's different.'

Jeet raised an eyebrow, and Raj was struck again at how similar she was to Roop. He felt suddenly besieged with these two women on either side of him.

'When the time came, I wasn't even able to draw my kirpan.'

He felt a sudden seizure of terror, remembering the way the man's arm had felt around his chest. The way he had looked at him with nothing but malice and hatred in his eyes – no mercy, just pure darkness.

'You were ready to draw it back at Heera's house,' said Jeet.

'There will be other times, Raj,' added Roop softly, and the chance of it made a shiver escape down his spine.

'Exactly,' said Jeet. 'Listen to your sister – though if I may observe, the two of you look absolutely nothing alike.'

Raj and Roop exchanged a quick glance in the dim light of the candle.

'People have said that in the past …' said Roop evasively.

Jeet narrowed her eyes. Raj gulped. Jeet Kaur didn't seem like someone easily fooled, and he could already see the suspicion building in her eyes.

'Strange. But anyway. Roop Kaur's point is the right one. So you're a bit of a rubbish fighter, so what? We can train you up.'

'You're going to train me?'

Jeet raised her eyebrow again. 'Why do you sound so surprised?'

Raj coughed nervously. 'I just thought …'

'I am woman who has lived on her own in these forests for the last three years. You think I would still be here if I didn't know how to swing a sword?'

She leaned closer and tapped the side of Raj's neck, tracing his carotid artery. 'If I didn't know exactly where to strike?'

Raj gulped. 'Sorry.'

'I'll let it go this time. But if you ever try to undermine me again …'

She left her threat unfinished, blowing out the candle she was holding and sending them all back into darkness.

'I really like her,' whispered Roop in his ear, and he could tell she was smiling.

He shuffled nervously onto his sleeping mat, not knowing whether Jeet's presence on the mat next to him made him feel safer or more in danger than ever.

CHAPTER NINE

The Night Before Battle

By the time Raj awoke the next morning, the rest of the campsite had already begun its daily activities. It took him a moment to pick up what was different about this morning, and he realised, achingly, that he missed Mehtab's presence. He knew Mehtab would never have let him sleep in until late morning, even if he was recovering from bloody wounds on his face and hands. He slipped away from the quiet bustling of the site and headed towards the small pond that Resham had shown him on his first day. He washed carefully, trying to avoid getting his bandages wet and dressed in a loose kurta he had borrowed from the washing line.

He needed to think of a plan. They needed desperately to find a *baaj* and go back home. That was the sensible thing to do. It would be stupid and dangerous to wade back into a battle with these people, even if he did feel bad about his role in Mehtab's capture. He had already proven his lack of ability to fight and his cowardice. The best thing in everyone's interest would be for him and Roop to leave.

And yet … he kept thinking about the bearded time traveller that had sent them here. The way he had showed him what must have been Resham's notebook. The way he had said there would be a lesson for him to learn.

'Well,' he muttered to himself. 'I guess I'm just as much a failure as I always thought I was.'

'Talking to yourself?'

Raj let out an undignified yelp and somehow managed to trip over his own feet, landing sprawled on the forest floor, a flash of pain shooting up his hand.

'Oh God,' said Jeet, offering her hand to him. 'I didn't mean to scare you that much. I only wanted to ask if you were up for some training.'

Raj got to his feet and dropped her hand immediately, cradling his injury protectively to his chest.

'I'm not quite up to it. I think I should rest for a couple of days–'

Jeet snorted and then held her hand over her mouth apologetically. 'Sorry, I am just surprised. You don't want to go after the guy who gave you that scar? You wanna know what I did to the man who gave me this one?'

She gestured to the side of her face, and Raj nodded despite himself.

'I got this when I first ran away from home. I was taken in by this family who agreed to let me sleep with the cows if I did some chores on their farm. Anyway, it was a great arrangement until one of the sons came looking for more – when I tried to fight him off, he gave me this.'

Raj looked down at his feet, feeling unable to meet her eyes. 'I'm so sorry.'

'Why are you apologising?' she said, laughing. 'You won't feel sorry for me once you know what I did ... behind the cowshed was a shallow trench, and inside it there lived a snake … very poisonous. Everyone was too scared to go near it. I knew, though, that it was harmless – until it was provoked. I wasn't scared when it wrapped itself around my arm – it's like it knew what we were going to do … I waited until the boy was sleeping, and I slipped it into his bed. He was screaming most of the night. It was a gradual paralysis – he couldn't even move his eyes in their sockets by the time the poison had done its job. The snake escaped. I wish I'd had a chance to say thank you and goodbye.'

Raj was stunned; he swallowed nervously. 'Please remind me never to cross you.'

She laughed at that and punched his shoulder playfully. 'Now come on, try and hit me.'

Raj was exhausted, but he got the feeling that Jeet wouldn't give up. They were only a few minutes in when he realised he was completely out of his depth. Jeet's feet moved faster than any he had ever seen, maybe even faster than Mehtab's, whipping from one position to another before he'd even had time to form a fist. Once, he managed to catch one of her shoulders, and he celebrated for a split second before she kicked him hard in the shins and then pushed him to the ground.

'Ouch!'

'You're pretty terrible. This is going to take a while.'

They were at it until midday when she finally agreed to let him limp back to the campsite to get some food. His stomach growled as he downed a bowl of *dhaal*, Roop watching him in amusement.

'I've never seen you that excited about *dhaal*.'

'You won't believe what Jeet just put me through.'

'Trust me; I can. I did the same thing with her earlier. She said I show potential.'

Raj rolled his eyes. 'Are we going to be competitive about this like we were back in Oxford?'

Roop's lips twitched.

'What's an Oxford?'

Raj avoided jumping this time as Jeet took a seat on the ground next to him.

'How do you creep up on people like that?!' he asked.

'I'll teach you tomorrow. You both stomp a lot. Living in the forest, you have to learn light-footedness, or you end up being something else's lunch.'

'Hurry up and eat; we're meeting in the main tent to start planning after this,' Vikram said, sitting down opposite them. 'We should start thinking about making a move tonight. To get our Jathedar back.'

Raj felt the same numbing, icy fear in his chest. All he could see was the guard's eyes and then Mehtab's. He took a steadying breath.

'Raj Singh, are you okay?' asked Vikram.

'He's fine! He's just had a few rounds with Jeet.' Resham laughed jovially, clapping him on the back and settling in between him and Jeet. 'She will make a warrior out of you.'

'He's already a warrior,' said Jeet boldly, reaching behind Resham to slap Raj on the back too. He winced.

When they shuffled into the central tent, Raj felt the same pang he had felt in the morning. Vikram and Kashmir stood at the front, the same spot Mehtab had been standing in. He sat down on the hard floor, all his muscles straining. He thought longingly of the softness of his bed again, of clean sheets, and most of all, of safety.

'So, as you all know, we have reason to believe that Mehtab Singh, our Jathedar, is still alive.'

'Of course, he is,' said one of the women at the front. 'They'll all be afraid of going near him.'

A few others murmured agreement.

'So it is time to bring him home. Kashmir Singh and I have thought of a plan.'

Resham leaned in closer to Raj. 'They said I shouldn't be involved in planning this time; apparently, my plans are too reckless, though the only reason the previous one failed was that you went back for a b*aaj*.'

Raj squirmed in embarrassment and guilt. 'I didn't know.'

Resham smiled. 'I'm joking. I understand – the bird of Guru Gobind Singh Jee being trapped by the Turks. It made me angry too. Don't worry; we'll go back – get Mehtab and the b*aaj*.'

'– so it's going to take all of the fauj. We will all travel under cover of darkness, and at midnight we will meet Narayan Singh's Jatha – and then –'

'They will feel the full force of the Khalsa,' finished Vikram, holding his *kirpan* – their *kirpan* with the peacocks – tightly. Raj looked at the *kirpan* and then at Resham's pocket – from which the edges of his battered notebook were just visible – the account of a single Singh appearing when all hope seemed lost. That was Vikram he realised with a sudden certainty. That account may well be written about the battle they were all riding into.

'Do you think this is a good idea?' he asked Resham nervously. 'What if they're prepared, and we all get killed?'

'The battle is fought and won in the mind way before you even reach the battlefield – do you remember, Mehtab Singh told you that in the forest?'

'I do,' said Raj, 'but I don't want anything to happen to you …'

Resham Singh shrugged. 'There are worse things than dying, Raj Singh.'

Raj gulped.

'A messenger has just arrived,' said one of the Singhs from the tent entrance. A few minutes later, a younger Singh rushed into the tent. He couldn't have been more than a teenager, a light, wispy beard just beginning to grow from his chin.

'*Waheguru Jee Ka Khalsa, Waheguru Jee Ki Fateh.*' His voice was deeper than Raj had expected.

Once they had responded to his greeting, he cleared his throat as though about to reel off something from memory. He said, 'I have been sent from the Jatha of Narayan Singh. He has praised your courage and fortitude in seeking to get Mehtab Singh back from the hands of the enemy. He has sent out spies who have been watching the fort, and he has asked me to pass on the position of the guards to you after I have delivered my message. His spies have also seen something else – women and children stolen from the local village are now also being held in the deepest rooms in this very fort. Rumour has it that they will be delivered to the evil tyrant, Ahmed Shah Abdali, in the coming days. Narayan Singh implores you all to be ready to fight to the death for the freedom of these innocent people – he says he will try to gather more forces in the coming days and that we will need to strike with all our might tonight.'

There was a silence before a chorus of war cries filled the tent at almost deafening volume.

'Pass on to Narayan Singh that we stand ready to fight shoulder-to-shoulder with you all and that it would be our honour to attain *shaheedi* by your sides.'

The boy put his palms together and bowed to Vikram and Kashmir.

'Resham, get our guest some food and water. I'm sure he has more messages to deliver.'

Resham stood and led the boy out of the tent.

Jeet stood up. 'We cannot waste a moment. Permit me to lead one of the groups.'

Vikram nodded without hesitation. 'Thank you for joining us – but everyone here must realise that there is a strong possibility none of us will return.'

Jeet's eyes flashed. 'I would consider it a personal failure if I did.'

Raj tapped Roop on the elbow. 'Come with me, quickly.'

He led her out to the edge of the campsite, back to the stream where he had washed this morning.

'We have to get out of here.'

'What?'

'Roop, you can't honestly be wanting to go into battle with these guys? Trust me, I've been – we're going to be totally useless. We'll be killed in the first minute–'

'So your plan is to run away? To abandon them? You realise they are the only reason we're alive right now?'

'Well, they are also the reason I almost got killed–'

'Whose side are you on, Raj? We have to try and help. We can tie bandages, or make food, or something – anything! We could get the baaj this time! I'm not going to sneak away in the middle of the night like some coward–'

'Wow,' he said softly. 'So that's what you think of me.'

Roop sighed, rubbing her face with her hand. 'I didn't mean it like that, I swear.'

He knew he was a coward; he had known since the moment he had turned away from Mehtab and ran away into the dark. But it still hurt to hear her say it.

'You're right,' he said finally. 'You're brave, and I'm not-'

'Raj–'

'No.' he said, lifting his hand. 'I get it … I agree with you. I'm cowardly, depressed, useless–'

'You lost somebody you really loved, Raj. You've carried that grief around for so long. You need to learn how to put it down, how to–'

'You don't understand – maybe you will once your mum dies – but until then, you won't get it.'

Roop jerked backwards as though he had physically struck her.

He felt his stomach drop, guilt and shame flooding him with a sudden and powerful force.

'No, I didn't mean it like that, Roop –'

But it was too late; he saw something shift and then switch off in her eyes. She brushed hair away from her face, an achingly familiar gesture that felt suddenly hostile.

'Stay away from me.'

'Please …'

But she had already left his side. He collapsed next to the pool of water, watching his reflection as tears slid down his face.

All day, the Sikhs made preparations for war. The first raid of the Lahore fort was nothing compared to the activity that began as soon as the messenger moved on to find his next audience. A group of Sikhs began to make food, more Sikhs began to clean the rust from long iron swords, some of which were too heavy for Raj to even carry; a map of the fort was drawn and then re-drawn in the sand, and groups of Sikhs in varying configurations stood around it, pointing out different points of attack, conversing and debating about who would be best able to lead the captives to safety, and who would stay behind to die.

The talk about death was what disturbed Raj the most. It seemed like an unimportant detail – the fact that many people would never return – as though the outcome of the battle didn't really matter as long as the battle took place.

They cared about saving the women and children, but beyond that, death was as inevitable as it was uninteresting. Raj wandered from group to group, watching the flurry of activity, a feeling of disquiet and fear weighing on his chest like stone. He wished he could be like Resham, humming shabads under his breath, laughing joyfully and without care. Or like Vikram, who was more serious and stuck close to Kashmir Singh, who was now the oldest Sikh in the Jatha and seemed like the most trusted. Even Roop, sticking close with Jeet, helping to gather medical supplies to take with them, wore the same look of detached determination. Raj wasn't sure that he recognised her anymore; he certainly didn't recognise the cold, emotionless way she looked whenever they happened to make eye contact.

As night began to fall, everyone took to their own sleeping areas, and Raj observed the last of their pre-battle rituals with interest. Vikram led a jaap of Gurbani, which sounded like dasam bani with some of the other Sikhs, a small fire lit to provide light and warmth in the cooling night. Kashmir Singh whispered softly to Bijali, who Raj was pleased to see had escaped their previous raid on the fort unscathed. Jeet was playing an old Taus, a long stringed instrument with a head shaped like a peacock. At first, she played softly, in tune with the chanting of the other Sikhs, until Vikram called her forward and gestured to her to play louder. Raj sat down on a long, wooden log near the group and closed his eyes.

He felt every hair on his body rise as the gurbani washed over him, the sound of the taus strong against the low wind, which began to blow softly through the forest. As the wind blew past his ears, he felt rather than heard the sound of thousands of voices – way more than the number that had currently assembled. It was as though he was already on a battlefield. He closed his eyes tighter, not wanting to let the vision go because there was something strong and filled with light leading them. No – not something, someone – a force more powerful than anything he had ever seen. He couldn't describe the shape under the light, but he desperately wanted to see it – and to be seen by it, to feel it. He knew instinctively it was Guru Gobind Singh Ji, and if he squeezed his eyes tight enough, he could make out a kalgi – and on the shoulder of the figure, he could see a *baaj*.

Kashmir ordered everyone to get a couple of hours of rest before they started riding out. Some Sikhs continued the *paat* while others retired to their sleeping mats. Raj waited until it was quiet, then he picked up an old, ragged rucksack he had borrowed from the supply tent. He had filled it with *sholey* earlier in the day and packed Jeet's flask, which he hoped she would not miss. It was totally, and suffocatingly dark in the forest, but he felt his way as best as he could, placing his palm flat against each of the trees he passed. He could make out a glint of moonlight in the smaller clearing with the stream, and he made his way over to it. In the light of the moon, he could make out his reflection.

Raj Singh, running away, he thought. He wondered what Bhagat would say. He would have wanted him to stay behind and fight, to be a hero. Like Roop. Like Heera. Like Arjun. He was surrounded by those people, he realised suddenly, and all he had inside him was fear. He turned away from the water and had begun to make his way through the next set of trees when there was a low cough behind him.

'Leaving for the battle already?'

Raj spun around. It was Vikram. He stood calmly next to the pool of water, his hands folded behind him, the light of the moon glinting on the *kirpan* – their *kirpan*.

'I was just–'

'You know Resham and I have a wager on how many Turks we can take down. I assume you're trying to get ahead of both of us? Always the quiet ones you have to watch out for …'

Raj hung his head in shame. 'You know I'm trying to run away.'

Vikram shook his head. 'No way. I don't believe that – one of the others maybe I would believe, but not you, Raj Singh.'

Raj felt tears building up in his eyes. 'I'm the biggest coward in this whole entire forest. I don't deserve your kindness.'

'You're destined for greatness. You just don't believe it yet.'

'That is you – not me,' said Raj, wishing he could tell Vikram about Resham's diary, that hundreds of years from now, it would be written that it was Vikram who was the last Sikh standing. Just when the enemy thought they had won, he would be the defiant one who rallied the Sikhs to fight one more time.

'No, it's you.'

'Trust me; it's you.'

'Are we going to keep doing this all night?' said Vikram, smiling. 'Or are you ready to come back to the campsite with me?'

'I'm scared of dying. I don't want to die.'

'What's scary about it?'

'It will hurt–'

'Only for a very short time – after that, it will be a pure, eternal bliss.'

'For you maybe – I'm a sinner –'

'You don't think Guru Jee loves you just the same?'

'I don't think Guru Jee has a plan for me at all.'

'They sent you here, to us, didn't they?'

'But I don't understand why. I am not special – I have no talent – I'm not brave.'

'It takes more courage to be afraid, and to fight than to have no fear at all.'

Raj was silent at that.

Vikram walked up to him and put a hand on his shoulder. 'I'm not going to force you, Raj Singh, just to say this – there are a few moments in our life which have the power to define who we are. This is that moment for you. You can be afraid and run, or you can be afraid and stay – and between those options is all the difference in the world. But either way, you don't stop being my brother, and either way, the Guru still loves you. Like how a father may scold a misbehaving child but still takes him to his chest after.'

Raj swallowed a rising lump in his throat and found suddenly he could not speak. Vikram held out a hand, and Raj slid off his rucksack and handed it to him.

'We'll need these supplies tonight when we ride out.' said Raj softly.

Vikram's face broke into a brilliant smile.

CHAPTER TEN

The Return to Lahore

A few hours later, the first rays of dawn began to break across the sky. Raj tossed and turned on his sleeping mat, wanting to wake Roop so he could beg her to forgive him, wanting to nudge Jeet and ask her to teach him some more ways to avoid getting killed, wanting to run to Kashmir and beg him to reconsider the whole operation. He thought about Mehtab and had the image of a lion prowling a cage too small for him.

When it was finally time to leave, the group was quiet, subdued in their own thoughts and prayers. Horses were in short supply, so some Sikhs had to double up. Raj was paired with Resham, who rode his horse erratically, moving fast to be at the front of the group and then urging his horse to go slower to allow him to whisper jokes with those travelling at the back of the group. Raj's exhausted body eventually gave in to sleep, waking only when he felt a sharp elbow in his rib.

'What is it with you and always falling asleep on horseback? We're riding into battle here! You're supposed to be singing a good battle song or telling me a story about a good, bloody, historical battle!'

'I don't know any,' said Raj honestly. 'Sorry.'

Resham sighed. 'I've brought my notebook. Do you think it's true, what you said before when I told you about it, that someone might want to read it a hundred years from now?'

'It depends,' said Raj. 'On how good the story is.'

'I reckon it'll be a good one if I survive to be able to write about it.'

Raj managed a smile. 'I think so too.'

The trees began to thin as they retraced the route to the old fort. As the surroundings began to take on a sense of familiarity, so too began a feeling of paralysing fear, riding down Raj's back like an animal, making him stiff and numb on the back of the horse. When it was time to dismount, his back ached; he moved his numb toes slowly in his trainers to regain some feeling like Mehtab had taught him. Instinctively, they gathered around Kashmir Singh, carrying the longest sword Raj had ever seen.

'We're not sneaking in this time. We're not here to take food or supplies. We're here for a divine mission. A noble cause.' His voice was quiet, barely more than a whisper, but it felt like the only sound in the whole world. Raj felt goosebumps erupt over his skin, and his heartbeat accelerated. He sneaked a glance over at Roop, wanting to make amends in case … he didn't finish the thought. Instead, he stared down determinedly at his feet, willing himself not to be sick.

Kashmir Singh outlined the plan again, and though Raj had heard it dozens of times over the evening, he listened hard, feeling scared suddenly that he hadn't understood properly.

'Are we ready?' asked Kashmir, looking around. 'We're not hiding anymore.'

Someone – and he couldn't tell who – let out the loudest Jakaara Raj had ever heard in his life, and he responded shouting at the top of his lungs – letting out the fear, the frustration, the exhaustion. And then they rode again to the edge of the clearing. Vikram raised a conch shell to his mouth and blew a signal that they had arrived: to both the Turks in the fort and Narayan Singh's jatha in the distance.

Vikram turned his horse towards Raj and handed him the shell.

'If you need any help, blow into this, and someone will come.'

Vikram gave him a small nod and turned back towards the battlefield. He would be OK, Raj reminded himself. Vikram and Resham had to have survived this for Resham to write about it in his diary. He kept repeating this to himself as he gazed out across the field in between them – what would soon become a battlefield. A couple of seconds later, the rusty gates opened with an almost ear-splitting creak, and the morning's silence was ruptured for a second time. And then came the sound of hundreds of hooves – more and more mounted Turk soldiers came pouring out of the fort entrance.

Raj gulped. He knew the odds would not be great, but he hadn't expected this.

He turned to Resham and saw he was smiling.

'*Sava lakh* – Raj – remember, one of us is worth 125,000 of them.'

Raj nodded, wishing desperately he could borrow some of his courage. Even from a distance, Raj could make out the sneers of the Turks. They were laughing at them. He thought how the Sikhs must have looked to them- ragged, exhausted, hungry. Courage is not the absence of fear, he reminded himself, just the belief that other things are more important.

Suddenly, he felt something squeeze his arm; he turned to see Roop reaching out with her hand. He took it without thinking and squeezed hard. She smiled, and he knew his apology had been accepted.

'We are giving you one chance,' shouted the Turk guard. Raj felt fear constricting his throat; it was the same guard who had grabbed him when he was about to leave. He could almost feel his thick fingers around his neck, his short knife slicing through his face. 'Surrender now, and we will make your death painless.'

'No, tyrant. We're giving you one chance – release the innocent women and children you have imprisoned, and we will give you a quick death!' retorted Vikram.

The guard laughed. 'We have nothing left to say to each other. We'll remove your kind from the face of the Earth. There are just a few dozen of you and many hundreds of us.'

'We have never been the kind to run from those odds; ask your ancestors about it.'

The guard stopped sneering, anger filling his face as he shouted in a foreign language, and the soldiers began to canter forward. In the distance, another battle horn erupted.

Raj whipped his head to the eastern edge of the forest and saw more men and women, some mounted and others walking. On their shoulders was a battle standard – the Khalsa battle standard.

'Narayan Singh's Jatha!' said Jeet happily. 'Finally.'

The enemy's smiles faltered as the odds became almost even. And Raj thought – as ragged, tired, and hungry as the Sikhs looked, there was a vibrancy about them that he couldn't quite define in his head. They had come prepared to die he realised suddenly, that was the difference.

Resham sighed, his red-rimmed eyes hardening. 'Enough wasting time, Vikram Singh; it's time to show them what we are made of.'

'I couldn't agree more.'

And then they were riding into battle, Resham's horse almost flying. Raj was clinging hard to Resham's shoulders, when without warning, Resham jumped down from the horse mid-gallop, landing gracefully on his feet. He drew two swords from his scabbard, and the enemy was on him. Raj grabbed the horse's reins desperately, trying to direct it around to the side of the fort. The sounds of the battle were louder than anything he had ever heard – the sound of metal against metal as soldiers crashed against each other, the dull thud of the sword, the screams of pain, of anger. And so much blood. Everywhere Raj looked, there was blood. He didn't know where to focus his vision or how to stay aware of his surroundings as they blurred all around him. He urged his horse forwards; in his peripheral vision, he could see that some of the Sikhs were following him, as had been planned.

He felt bile rising in his mouth as he realised why the ground was getting darker beneath him. His vision blurred even more as he saw limbs without owners – sprays of blood exploding in the sky –

'Watch out Raj!'

He turned around, raising his rusty sword and blocking an attack from a stocky guard, his bright green eyes gleaming from his iron helmet. Raj wanted to beg him to stop, but of course, they were in battle, and it was kill or be killed, so he pushed back as hard as he could. The guard lost his balance, almost falling off his horse, but before he could fall, Jeet raised her sword and sliced his head cleanly from his body. Raj turned away and rode faster than he thought possible.

This was what battle was, he realised suddenly; it was nothing like the movies. There was just blood and pain and chaos. As he reached his destination, more guards fell on him; he raised his sword with a sudden determination to block blows. He yelled out for help to the Sikhs behind him – and then Jeet's white horse was riding forward, and under her sword, the guards fell one by one.

'Go!' yelled Jeet. 'There are more of them coming. Get inside!'

Raj yelled 'Let's go!' in English before he knew what he was saying, but it was too loud to hear him anyway. He looked around frantically for Roop and then grabbed her hand.

'We're going to have to get off our horses!' he said. 'We're too visible!'

He slid off his horse, falling into a crawl on the cold and hard ground. When they reached the stone sidewall of the fort, he stood up cautiously to look around – it was only him, Roop, and three other Sikhs that must have been from Narayan Singh's jatha as he didn't recognise them. None of the others had made it.

'What's the plan?' whispered one of the Sikhs, an older man. Raj realised he only had one arm, and he tried not to stare as he relayed it: they were to climb over the wall, head to the dungeons where rumours said the prisoners were trapped and release them. The man nodded, barking orders to the others.

'Stand back,' said Roop, reaching for the small sack of powder that Jeet had helped her make. She struck a match into the powder, throwing it at the wall. There was an explosion so loud it made Raj's ears ring. He closed his eyes, trying to get his sense of balance back.

'Come on! They're coming!'

They climbed through the rubble of the wall. A guard lay unconscious and bleeding on the other side of the red bricks. Raj saw Roop glance down at the body and her bottom lip trembled. He grabbed her hand again.

'We had to. Come on.'

Raj recognised the interior from their previous mission – the same square courtyard – deserted, with the supply tent in the middle, which he was sure they would have emptied. The rooms around the edge of the courtyard were also quiet, with no guards at any of them.

'This doesn't feel right …'

'Sikhs in the fort!'

Suddenly the courtyard was filled with the sound of arrows whistling through the air.

'Get under cover!' yelled Raj. The one-armed Sikh shoved them both under the courtyard awnings. Raj yelled for him to follow, but an arrow came from the sky and landed squarely in his chest. The Sikh looked down at the wooden arrow and then back up at Raj. And he smiled.

Raj stood transfixed; the man – with an arrow still protruding from his chest – had picked up his spear and turned, throwing it with all his force to the archer standing at the mouth of the fort, who fell immediately with a sickening thud.

'I know where they are!' yelled Roop in Raj's ear. They raced away from the dead guard and the one-armed Sikh towards a wooden door in the corner of the complex. Roop pulled more powder from her pocket.

Raj pushed himself against the door and yelled as loud as he could, 'Get away from the door! We've come to free you, but you need to stand right back!'

Another explosion later, they were inside a dim, windowless room. Rows and rows of women, blinking against the sudden assault of light, were sitting side by side. Some holding small children, others with arms wrapped around their knees.

'Come on!' said Roop. 'We need to move now!'

One of the women, dressed in a long, pink salwar kameez, stood up. 'Who are you people?!'

But before they could answer, another girl had stood up. 'You're the Khalsa!'

Raj looked down at his kara, on a hand holding a sword, and felt a fierce sense of pride fill his heart.

'Yes. And we're here to get you out of here.'

The women suddenly scrambled to get up, gathering meagre belongings, grabbing children's hands, some of whom started to cry as the sounds of battle seemed to grow closer outside.

'Roop, you know the plan, right? The same side entrance and keep running – like your life depends on it.'

'Because it does.'

'Yes.'

'Where are you going?!'

'Mehtab- and then back for the baaj – if it's still there.'

Roop nodded, understanding.

Raj watched as they made their way to the side entrance. The other Sikhs had finished off the archers, but Raj knew it was just a matter of time before more Turks came rushing back. He turned back to the doors lining the courtyard and tried one door after another; they were either locked or empty, and he knew instinctively that Mehtab would be kept in the most secure location of them all. He climbed a set of creaky stairs to a second floor, keeping his sword close to him. On the way, he spotted a shield lying discarded on the floor, and he picked it up, holding it close to his body. At the very end of the corridor, he could see a door with metal bars. Bingo.

'Mehtab Singh, if you're in there, stand back from the door!'

There was only silence. Raj felt desperation building in him. 'Mehtab Singh! Can you hear me?'

No response. A tear slipped down his face. He was too late. *Mehtab had died, and it was all because of me,* he thought. *How had I thought I could be the one to rescue him?*

'Raj Singh?'

Raj grabbed the bar so hard he felt it would break off. 'Mehtab, you're alive!'

'Well, it sounds like it doesn't it?! What the hell are you doing in here when the battle is outside?'

'I've come to get you –'

'Don't be stupid – save the women; there's women and children here –'

'We have them already – it's just you. Stand back from the door.'

'What –'

'Stand back!'

He waited until he heard shuffling footsteps receding and then pulled out the pouch of powder in his pocket. A third explosion and Raj coughed as the smoke cleared to reveal Mehtab. He looked terrible. His clothes were dirty, covered in dirt and blood. His leg looked bad, infected. His beard and eyes were wilder than ever. His dastaar was askew, hanging around his shoulders.

'I won't be able to run,' was the first thing he said.

'Come on,' said Raj impatiently.

Mehtab shook his head. 'A soldier must carry his own weight in battle.'

Raj grabbed Mehtab's arm, wondering at his own daring, and put it around his shoulders. 'I'll help you like you helped me that day in the forest. When I couldn't get off the horse.'

They limped out of the room, down the creaking wooden stairs.

'Behind you!' growled Mehtab, and before Raj even knew what he was doing, he had swung his sword blindly behind him. It made impact and a Turk guard fell, his eyes glassy as pools of blood spilled from his neck.

'Good aim,' said Mehtab approvingly. Raj felt his stomach turn, and he pulled Mehtab quickly towards the exploded side entrance of the fort. They needed to move fast, across the exposed battlefield and into the safety of the trees.

'No,' said Mehtab heavily as they reached the broken wall. 'I can't go any further, and I am slowing you down. Go without me.'

'A battle is won or lost in the mind long before it's ever fought on the field,' said Raj softly. 'Remember when you told me that?'

'There was I thinking you never listened to a word I said. We're not getting out of this alive, you know – they'll follow us into the forests – they won't stop until we're gone.'

'Have you given up faith?'

'Never,' said Mehtab, scowling. 'I would die a thousand times before I ever did that.'

'Well then, we just have to keep going.'

113

Mehtab narrowed his eyes at Raj and then nodded. Raj grabbed Mehtab's arm. In the distance, the sound of battle waged on, and they continued their painfully slow limp. Raj heard the horses galloping towards them and closed his eyes for a second before looking up at the new group of Turks now surrounding them. Their faces were covered in dirt and sweat, their armour hanging loose from their bodies, swords dripping with blood.

'You think we would just let you escape with our prisoners? We'll hunt you to the ends of the universe!' yelled the Turk in the front; it was the same guard he had met on his first trip into the fort. He gulped. Raj counted twenty of them.

'Can you hear the quietening of the battle? All the Sikhs are dead. You're the last ones.' he taunted, leaning forward on his horse.

'No,' said Raj. 'That's not possible.'

'Oh yes – even the women, you thought we would just let them go? We will kill them all for daring to escape.'

One of the guards dismounted, raising his sword. Raj picked up his own sword, trying to keep Mehtab upright at the same time. This was the end, surely. But it couldn't be, he reminded himself. Resham's notebook had said Vikram would be here. He would fight until the end and emerge victorious. He tried to scan the horizon, but the Turk was right – the sounds of battle were quietening, and he couldn't see a single Khalsa battle standard still upright. A feeling of hopelessness came over him in a wave, and his legs suddenly felt unsteady.

'I will make this death slow. I will enjoy it,' said the guard.

Raj prayed harder than he had in his life, and Mehtab growled in his ear. 'Give me a sword.'

Raj handed him his rusty iron sword and pulled his own kirpan from his gatra. He felt in his pocket for any more of the powder, but he knew already there was none; instead, his fingers closed around – the conch shell!

He pulled it out of his pocket and blew as hard as he could. The guards all began to laugh.

'There are no Sikhs left, you stupid idiot! Are you not understanding what is happening here?'

Raj released his grip on Mehtab's shoulders and moved to stand in front of him.

'What do you think you're doing?' growled Mehtab. 'Let me at him first.'

'No,' said Raj softly. 'Stay back.'

'Raj Singh!'

The guards whipped around, and there was Resham Singh and Vikram Singh riding towards them like the wind, closely followed by Roop.

Resham and Vikram made quick work of the guards, moving with so much ferocity that they almost didn't appear real – it was like watching a movie on fast forward. Raj took advantage of the distraction and pulled Mehtab behind some of the rubble remnants of the fort wall.

'Stay here,' he said.

'I'm not hiding from any battle,' retorted Mehtab.

'You can't walk!'

Mehtab couldn't seem to think of a response to that, so Raj turned away.

Vikram Singh looked towards him. 'More Turks are coming this way! We need to get to the forest to regroup–'

But he never got to finish his sentence; he fell flat on his face. Raj heard a strangled scream, as if from a distance, but he realised suddenly that it was him. Vikram was bleeding out, an arrow sticking out of the back of his white chola.

Raj looked up; the guard was carrying a bow and arrow, sneering at him.

'You coward!' screamed Raj. 'Firing while his back was turned–'

'You're calling me a coward? The same one who left behind his friend to die in the fort?'

Raj looked around, Resham was also lying face down in the grass a few metres away, but he could see his fingers moving. Roop was suddenly nowhere to be seen. He could hear Mehtab trying to crawl over to him. This wasn't supposed to be how it ended, he thought desperately. Vikram was supposed to be leading the resistance. He was supposed to be rallying the troops. Raj looked down at his *kirpan*, the same *kirpan* as Vikram's …

The realisation was sudden. The Singh with the peacock *kirpan* – the one who Resham had written about – it wasn't Vikram. It was Raj.

Raj raised his *kirpan* and the conch shell one last time and blew with all his might.

The few Turks left were laughing now, clapping each other on the back. Soon they would finish off the wounded.

The guard was still watching Raj, the ugly sneer remaining on his face.

'Are you ready to fight me now, little boy? Are you ready to meet your maker?'

Raj raised his *kirpan*. 'Come and find out.'

The guard charged at him, and though he delivered multiple blows, Raj couldn't feel any of them. Raj raised his *kirpan*, trying to block and attack as best he could. He looked up at the sky, thought fiercely about Bhagat and home. And then out of the ruined fort flew a *baaj*, and at the same time, the sound of a *jakaara* filled Raj's ears, and it was the most beautiful sound he had ever heard.

The guard dropped his sword and turned. The remnants of the Sikh jatha, led by Jeet on her beautiful white horse, charged towards them. The guards fell like dominos, slayed under her vengeful sword. Raj raised his own *kirpan*, and only when the guard had turned back towards him did he plunge it deep into the man's chest.

He staggered away from them, falling backwards into the dying grass of the battlefield.

'Raj!'

It was Roop, holding the *baaj* on her arm. 'It just came to me!'

Raj smiled and then looked down at his body. It was covered in blood.

Roop screamed. 'Raj!'

And then Mehtab was pulling his head onto his lap.

'You fought like a true Khalsa,' he said. 'You are not of this world. I was right all along. Your brother would have been proud.'

Raj grabbed Mehtab's hand. 'So would yours.'

'The women, the children?' Raj asked, his throat feeling like it was constricting.

'They're safe,' said Roop, her voice trembling. 'They'll be deep in the forests by now.'

Resham limped over, holding his ripped chola to a wound on his neck.

'Raj, THE general is here. They're coming this way.'

'You mean Baba Deep Singh Ji?!'

Resham nodded, a small smile spreading across his exhausted face. 'You saved us all by blowing the horn. You can't die without seeing them. Look!'

Raj turned around, and riding towards him was a tall man, his long white beard just like the one in the paintings. Baba Deep Singh Ji. Raj tried to make out his face, but the sun was now beating too strong in his eyes. The Baaj flapped its wings. Roop took his hand. And then everything went black.

Raj opened his eyes; he was in a lush, green garden. The environment was so much a contrast to the barren battlefield he had arrived from that he had to blink a few times to allow his eyes to adjust to the new surroundings. The edges of the garden were shrouded in mist as if the whole stretch of greenery was suspended in mid-air. It took a moment for him to realise he was not alone. The old man – the time traveller

– worked in a corner, busily tending to a red rose bush. He wasn't wearing his long leather jacket. Instead, he was wearing a worn, brown Kurta, his hands in a pair of gardening gloves.

Raj didn't know where to start. Hadn't he dreamed of this moment feverishly for the last few days? He had thousands of questions dancing in his brain, but in the end, there was only one that seemed to matter.

'Why me?'

The man looked up and smiled. 'I was waiting for you to come around. Time travel is not for everyone; I must confess that I was starting to worry.'

'How did you do that – please don't be cryptic –'

'Some things are not to be understood, only accepted. I work for the one who turns the cosmos, who holds the world's notion of time in one hand, the searcher of hearts, the lover of devotion.'

'And what's all this?' asked Raj, gesturing to the mist around them.

'It's the chaos of the world, never-ending, impenetrable. He owns all of this too. You've asked why I sent you there; I wanted to remind you of who you could be, who you already are becoming.'

'I'm nothing like those Singhs and Kaurs. I was so scared the whole time; I was going to run away–'

'The people making history rarely know they are doing it, Raj. That was the point – they too held grief, felt fear, loved deeply and truly. Yet they still strode into battle, spat

in the face of death because of the conviction that there was something else more important.'

Raj felt tears sliding down his face. 'I thought the Sikh in the book was Vikram Singh. But it wasn't. It was me.'

The man came over to him, and Raj saw he was barefoot on the grass. He reached out to put a hand on Raj's shoulder, and when it made contact with the worn material of his T-shirt, Raj felt light suddenly, as though an invisible, unknowable weight had been lifted from his shoulders.

'How does that even work?' asked Raj. 'How could it have been me, recorded in the past – I didn't exist yet?'

'That was the universe at play – the unfolding of Hukam. The Universe sent you where you both needed to go – and where you were needed. That's the way it's always been.'

Raj tried to wrap his mind around this. 'I haven't done my nitnem properly in years. I'm afraid Guru Jee will turn me away when I reach his door.'

'The house of Nanak is one of forgiveness, but you need to forgive yourself before you can ask the Guru for it. As Mehtab Singh said, the battle is first won or lost in your own mind.'

'I have to go back, don't I? To the present day?'

The old man smiled. 'There is no such thing as THE present day, just one version of it that Guru Jee has put you in.'

'Will they be okay? Mehtab? Resham? Jeet? Where's Roop?'

'Resham Singh is writing his account, Mehtab is healing for his next battle, and Jeet ... well, I am sure she is in the

forest somewhere, finding lost people and guiding them back to their purpose. As for Roop, she is by her mother's side, already back in Oxford.'

'Her mum's still going to die, isn't she?'

The man nodded. 'Death is a necessary transition. And as you saw, there are ways of becoming less afraid of it.'

Raj knew he was talking about Vikram, and his hands automatically found their kirpan and held on.

'But if we could go back in time, we could find the cancer earlier, and she would still be OK. We could go back to the day of Bhagat's accident ...'

He trailed off because the man was looking at him sadly, and he had watched enough sci-fi movies to know that he was asking for something impossible.

'Hukam unfolds and flows in mysterious ways, Raj Singh. It is what took me to you. I know you didn't believe in fate, but do you now see how we are connected in a million more ways than we could possibly imagine? If Bhagat hadn't died, would you have ended up on this battlefield for Resham Singh to write about?

Raj's mind felt like it was bending with the possibilities of what the old man was saying.

'Our time together has almost reached an end.'

'What am I supposed to do now?' Raj asked desperately. 'Are the men who were after you still in Oxford?'

The man laughed. 'They'll be chasing me elsewhere now. I think you are off the hook.'

Raj looked down at his hands and hesitated before saying, 'What if I don't want to go back?'

'You've still got some battles left in your life, Raj Singh. But whenever you feel alone, I want you to hold your kirpan like you are now and remember who fights along with you.'

Raj opened his mouth, but everything was fading away, like the memory of a dream. The old man raised a hand in farewell, and then for the second time, everything went black.

Oxford, Present Day

CHAPTER ELEVEN

Endings and Beginnings

'Can everyone be quiet for one minute?! I can't hear myself think!' Kirpal shouted from the front of the room.

Roop passed Raj some of the popcorn she had smuggled into the building.

'I think this is going to be a good meeting,' said Roop.

'Bets on how long before someone brings up Sikh speed dating again?' responded Raj.

They both chuckled. Raj settled more comfortably into his seat at the back of the lecture hall, enjoying being in Roop's company again, even if it was at the first Sikh Soc meeting of the term. They hadn't spent much time together since their adventure had come to an end. Roop's mother passed away in the middle of the summer; the funeral was in the same crematorium as Bhagat's had been. His mum had come with him, for which he was grateful because he didn't know any of Roop's extended family, and he didn't know how to offer comfort to complete strangers. Roop had tied her hair into a bun, and when he first saw her on that day, he thought there was something resolute in her expression that reminded him a lot of Jeet.

'How are you holding up?' he asked. 'I know it's a stupid question – I used to hate it when people asked me that after Bhagat.'

She hesitated. 'I never told you about this. But the day that Mum died, a few hours before – I had a dream about Jeet, Vikram, Resham, Mehtab – and others – they were all on horseback. When they saw me, they stopped, and Jeet got off her horse to tell me not to worry about Mum – that they were coming to take her to a better place. I think they're all together somewhere right now. And that's what keeps me going.'

'I read that Shaheed Sikhs come to take the faithful ones to the next resting place,' said Raj softly. 'It was kind of Jeet to come and let you know it's all going to be OK.'

Roop smiled. 'What's new with you, anyway?'

'I started doing my nitnem again.'

It had started the day after he woke up from their time in Punjab, a dull ache in his chest of longing, of memory, of wanting to crack a joke with Resham, of wanting to learn how to land a punch with Jeet, of wanting to seek Vikram's counsel. His feet seemed to have found their way to the Gurdwara on their own – he hadn't set foot inside since Bhagat's funeral. When he arrived, they were doing their morning nitnem, and he sat down unnoticed beside them. If he closed his eyes, they were back at the campsite – the chanting of *gurbani* filling all the empty spaces in his chest, and he realised then that they hadn't really left anything behind after all.

'And ...' he continued, 'I finally emptied Bhagat's bedroom. He wouldn't have wanted us to keep it as some kind of shrine. Mum was a bit hard to convince, but we actually sat down and had a conversation.'

'An actual conversation with your mother that didn't end in an argument or one of you storming out?!'

'I know. It's almost more surprising than travelling hundreds of years into the past.'

Roop didn't say anything, but he could see that she was smiling.

'I'm going to therapy.'

'Are you telling your therapist about the whole time travel thing?'

'I may omit some details to avoid being sectioned. And I still need to figure out how to return this *Chakram* ...'

'Maybe you should just keep it, as something to remember it all by.'

'I mean, I don't really see myself ever forgetting it.'

They both fell quiet as Kirpal stood up on a chair to call for order once again. The room gradually fell silent.

'Any ideas on events this year?'

Raj put his hand up before he could back out. Kirpal looked surprised for a second before pointing to him. 'Go ahead.'

'How about a sleep-out this winter? We could raise money for charity – in memory of the shaheeds.'

Kirpal's face broke into a smile. 'That is a *brilliant* idea. Can you take on organising the logistics?'

Raj nodded and turned to Roop. 'Will you help?'

'As if you could do it without me.'

Later on, as they filed out of the room, Roop turned to him. 'I just miss them all so much.'

'I know.' He gripped his *kirpan*, and his gaze fell onto their hazy reflection in the window. He couldn't make out any of their features except for the blueness of his dastaar and the glint of the kara on Roop's wrist.

'But I think they're still with us, in all the ways that matter."

The End.

Acknowledgements

This book is, of course, a work of fiction, but it draws its inspiration from the glorious and majestic history of the Sikh people. As such, I am hugely grateful to all the people in my life who have helped me to understand Sikhi better.

Thank you to my parents Jagpal Singh and Parmjit Kaur who told us *Sakhis* from our history every night before we went to bed as children. Thank you to my siblings Kam, Randeep, Sim, Upjeet, Arandeep and the wider Gill, Grewal and Kainth families who have led by example in teaching me that kindness, generosity, courage, and compassion are all qualities of the Khalsa.

A gratitude beyond words to Dyaal Singh, my grandfather, who first planted the seed of Sikhi in our family. He never got to read this story, but I feel like he would have loved it. Thank you also to my friends: Gurpreet, Dilpreet, Vicky, Amandip, Prableen, Harkaran, Damanjeet, Pannu and Asa – and so many others, for reading early drafts, making me laugh every day, and showing me an abundance of love and support.

Thank you to Narayan for reminding me of the power of a good story; you make my life brighter just by your presence.

Thank you to Ranveer Singh and Khalis House for believing in this story. I am so grateful for your guidance and kindness throughout this process.

Finally, none of this would have been possible without the blessings of Guru Nanak Dev Ji. May I be forgiven for the many mistakes made and made more worthy.